S0-BDQ-833

The time had come to stop playing games

Clutching her makeshift sarong to her body, Sharrel cautiously got up off the couch to stoke the fire in the shelter. She was just about to step over Tal, sleeping on the floor, when something closed, viselike, around her ankle.

His hand.

She looked down. His dark eyes stared up at her, as if his action had shocked him, too. As if he'd been impelled by an instinct beyond his control. Neither moved, neither spoke, yet messages arced between them.

And then she was sinking down beside him, the rough burlap falling open to expose the satin creaminess of her skin. He buried his face between her breasts, husky wordless sounds coming from his throat....

In high school **Lorena McCourtney** sold her first story, "Dad Has Plans," to *Alaska Sportsman* magazine. Now—hundreds of short stories later—she's excited about writing full-fledged romance novels. Her third Temptation, soon to come, will feature her favorite place, the stormy Oregon coast—but you'll catch a glimpse of it in *By Invitation Only*. Lorena also writes under the names Jocelyn Day and Lisa McConnell.

Books by Lorena McCourtney

HARLEQUIN TEMPTATION
73–NO STRINGS ATTACHED

These books may be available at your local bookseller.

Don't miss any of our special offers. Write to us at the following address for information on our newest releases.

Harlequin Reader Service
901 Fuhrmann Blvd., P.O. Box 1397, Buffalo, NY 14240
Canadian address: P.O. Box 603,
Fort Erie, Ont. L2A 9Z9

By Invitation Only

LORENA McCOURTNEY

Harlequin Books

TORONTO • NEW YORK • LONDON
AMSTERDAM • PARIS • SYDNEY • HAMBURG
STOCKHOLM • ATHENS • TOKYO • MILAN

Published August 1986

ISBN 0-373-25220-X

Copyright © 1986 by Lorena McCourtney. All rights reserved.
Philippine copyright 1986. Australian copyright 1986.
Except for use in any review, the reproduction or utilization of
this work in whole or in part in any form by any electronic,
mechanical or other means, now known or hereafter invented,
including xerography, photocopying and recording, or in any
information storage or retrieval system, is forbidden without
the permission of the publisher, Harlequin Enterprises Limited,
225 Duncan Mill Road, Don Mills, Ontario, Canada M3B 3K9.

All the characters in this book have no existence outside the
imagination of the author and have no relation whatsoever to
anyone bearing the same name or names. They are not even
distantly inspired by any individual known or unknown to the
author, and all incidents are pure invention.

The Harlequin trademarks, consisting of the words, TEMPTATION,
HARLEQUIN TEMPTATION, HARLEQUIN TEMPTATIONS,
and the portrayal of a Harlequin, are trademarks of Harlequin Enterprises
Limited; the portrayal of a Harlequin is registered in the United
States Patent and Trademark Office and in the Canada Trade
Marks Office.

Printed in Canada

1

SHARREL HATHAWAY TILTED her head, the movement sending a ripple through her red-gold hair. "Okay, that takes care of Cindy's arts-and-crafts project and your exercise class. Now tell me what has *really* put that sparkle in your eyes while I've been away these past six weeks." She appraised Nicole out of the corner of her eye. "A man?"

Nicole Dusek looked up from the cheese sauce she was stirring on the stove. She was twenty-eight, but with her heart-shaped face flushed and glowing beneath her pixie tousle of dark hair, she looked more like a wide-eyed teenager. Nicole's laugh was slightly breathless. "Is it that obvious?"

Shar stopped short in the act of tearing lettuce into bite-size pieces. "You mean you really have met someone who interests you?"

Nicole laughed again. "Shar, only a true friend like you could make it sound as if I've had a lineup of eager men just waiting for me to select the lucky one." Ruefully she added, "We both know that isn't exactly the way it's been."

"You could have had a lineup of eager men if you had let them know you existed instead of hiding behind closed doors," Shar argued staunchly.

Thinking of what Dave Dusek had done to Nicole made the old frustrated anger and disappointment well up in Shar. How *could* he have walked out on her and their daughter, Cindy, callously abandoning them for another woman? He was the last person in the world Shar would have expected to pull such a despicable stunt. Dave had always seemed such a predictable, even staid husband.

Shar bit back an unnecessary comment on Dave's sudden failings as a husband, venting her anger with a vicious rip at the lettuce. Nicole squeezed her arm lightly.

"I don't know what I'd have done without you to lean on through everything," Nicole said. Her soft voice quavered a little, the way it always did when emotion affected her.

They looked at each other for a long moment, the look encompassing the memory of Nicole's devastating brush with emotional and physical breakdown after her husband's betrayal. In spite of the happy glow in Nicole's eyes, Shar was conscious again of her friend's vulnerability and the fragility of her reconstructed life. If this new man did anything to hurt Nicole, she personally would pound him to a pulp, Shar vowed fiercely.

"So tell me all about this lucky guy." Shar turned back to top the salad with a sprinkling of Nicole's homemade croutons. "Who is he, where did you meet him, etcetera?"

"His name is Talcott O'Neal. He builds . . . well, buildings, I guess. He just moved up to the Portland area from southern Oregon a few months ago." Nicole poured the cheese sauce over the prepared casserole and slid the dish into the oven. "He bought out some other company that was about to go bankrupt."

Shar glanced up in surprise. "You mean he's O'Neal Construction, the company that took over that modular housing outfit? How did you ever happen to meet him?"

Shar had heard about the takeover of the nearly bankrupt company—before her business trip to southern California that had unexpectedly turned into an extended six weeks' absence. As a real estate broker she was always interested in that kind of news. She hadn't heard anything about O'Neal personally, but she knew his company had struck an extremely hard bargain in taking over the failing company. The knowledge gave her a moment of uneasiness. The last thing Nicole needed was to get involved with some hard ruthless guy who'd give her a rough time.

Nicole was answering Shar's question. "I went with the Andersons to look at one of the O'Neal Construction Company's model homes. The Andersons were thinking of buying one to use as a vacation cabin on their lot over on the coast. Tal was there and . . . things just happened." Nicole had a happy, slightly dazed, swept-off-her-feet look.

"What's he like?"

Nicole leaned against the kitchen counter, her eyes unfocused and dreamy. "He's dark haired, medium height, terrific athletic build. *Very* good-looking. Great dancer—"

Shar's uneasiness grew to dismay. Nicole could be describing her former husband. Surely she wouldn't choose a carbon copy of that cheater!

"Looks and dancing ability aren't everything," Shar cut in almost sharply.

"He's also interesting and fun. Very . . . mmm . . . masculine. But tender. He has a terrific smile and gorgeous green-brown eyes, and Cindy is crazy about him."

Still unconvinced, Shar folded her arms at her slim waist. "Why," she asked bluntly, "is Cindy crazy about him?"

Nicole tilted her dark head thoughtfully. "I think because he talks to her without being condescending, without that special tone some people have for children. And he listens to what she has to say. He's also given her some skiing lessons." Nicole laughed once more, a warm reassuring sound to Shar's ears after so many tears. "He offered to teach me, too, but you know how unathletic I am. Anyway, he and Cindy had a great time zooming down the slopes."

Talcott O'Neal rose a few notches on Shar's tough rating scale. She had considerably more respect for a person who gave of himself to a child than for one who tried to buy approval with presents and toys. However, she wasn't yet ready to grant that he deserved her best friend's affection.

"What kind of things do you do together?"

"We've driven out to the ski area at Mount Hood, of course, and we've been over to the coast. He's taken us to dinner at some nice places, and I've cooked for him here. We've gone dancing . . . and out to see the new baby elephant at the zoo. He fixed the brakes on my car—" Nicole broke off her listing of activities, eyes suddenly looking even more starry, if that was possible. "And I—I think I may be falling in love with him." Her breasts rose with her tremulous breath.

Shar didn't respond with wild approval. "How old is he? I suppose he's divorced?"

"He's thirty-two. He's never been married."

That information surprised Shar. Her green eyes narrowed. "Why not?"

Nicole wrinkled her pert nose at Shar's persistence. "I think he's been too busy with his career and business to have much time for the opposite sex. Like you," she added with a touch of teasing impertinence. "But now he's making sounds like a man who's ready to settle down with a family."

"You mean he's already asked you to marry him?"

"No," Nicole admitted. "But we've talked *around* marriage, and a woman can tell when a man is approaching the serious stage. Neither of us is seeing anyone else. We've gotten that far." She hesitated a moment, then amended the statement. "At least I don't think he's seeing anyone else."

Nicole took the lightly browned casserole out of the oven and carried it to the dining room table, which was set for two. Shar followed with the salad and home-baked rolls; seven-year-old Cindy was spending the night with a friend. Nicole placed the hot casserole on a hand-crocheted hot pad and motioned Shar to a seat. Shar murmured appreciatively once she'd tasted the casserole.

"Mmm, this is fantastic, Nikkie. Have you tried this out on—what did you say his name was? Talcott? This dish is surely the way to any man's heart."

"He does seem to like my cooking," Nicole admitted with modest pride. A little anxiously she added, "What do you think of him so far? I know you haven't met him yet, but from what I've told you?"

"He sounds terrific. I think you may have found a winner." Reluctantly, hating to say anything to dim the sparkle in Nicole's eyes, but a firm believer in facing reality, Shar added, "But don't be too quick to rush into something. You've known him only a few weeks, and even the world's worst louse can put on a good front for a few weeks."

"I know. He sounds almost too good to be true, doesn't he?" Nicole pushed a mushroom around on her plate, as if her appetite had suddenly lagged.

Shar gave Nicole a surprised glance over the rim of her wineglass. "That sounds rather cynical. Not like you at all."

"I've earned the right to be a little cynical, don't you think?" Nicole's usually sweet smile had an uncharacteristically bitter twist. "That's why I have a favor to ask of you."

"Ask away." In the brief silence that followed, Shar guessed that Nicole wanted her to make a few discreet inquiries into Talcott O'Neal's background. That wouldn't be difficult to do. Someone at the office probably already knew all that was worth knowing about the man. "I'll do anything I can to help. You know that."

"I want you to try to seduce him."

Shar choked on a crouton, gasped, took a sip of wine and finally shook her head in disbelief. "You can't be serious!"

"But I am. Dead serious."

"You actually want me to try to seduce the man you think you're falling in love with? Nikkie, hon, that is absolutely crazy. *Why?*"

"Shar, you know the answer to that." Nicole's tone was almost reproachful. Her lower lip wobbled. "I—I just couldn't face having another man do to me what Dave did. I just couldn't stand having it happen again." A liquid brightness wavered in her dark eyes. "I have to know before it's too late if he's the susceptible type."

Shar shook her head firmly. "Nikkie, you know there are a dozen flaws in that line of thinking."

Nicole didn't ask what the flaws were. She simply said stubbornly, "If he's immune to your best efforts at seduction, then I'll feel I can trust him."

The idea was so outrageous that Shar could do no more than shake her head again. "You make me sound like some femme fatale that no man but a saint could resist!"

"If you set your mind to it, you could have almost any man you wanted. You're beautiful, Shar. Dave said that you should have been in modeling or the movies instead of selling real estate."

Good old Dave Dusek had evidently had all sorts of thoughts lurking behind that bland insurance-company-executive exterior, Shar thought grimly. She could understand why Nicole wouldn't want to get tangled up with another man afflicted with Dave's wandering eye, but the idea of a seduction test was surely too incredible for serious consideration.

"Look at yourself," Nicole went on earnestly. She nodded toward the oval mirror on the far wall.

Reluctantly Shar's eyes met their jade reflection in the mirror. In the mellow lamplight she saw a tumble of red-gold hair, classic cheekbones with the light honey glow of a southern-California tan, a willowy slimness that emphasized the full roundness of her breasts beneath the loose velour pullover. She knew the combination was attractive. She saw it in men's admiring eyes and sometimes felt the acid of women's envious glances, as well.

But she had long ago learned to doubt the lasting value of a pretty face and attractive figure. She had seen in her mother's life that beauty insured neither happiness nor a faithful husband. Shar had already learned much the same lesson in her own life. She had no intention of trying to get by on physical assets.

Shar's eyes swung back to meet Nicole's serious expression. "If I'm so irresistibly attractive, how come I'm twenty-eight and unattached?" she inquired tartly.

Nicole's answer was prompt. "Because you're married to that high-powered real estate career of yours. You're so involved in setting up fourteen-way property trades—"

"You're exaggerating, you know."

Nicole smiled and shrugged her small shoulders, dismissing the specific numbers as immaterial. "You haven't time to get seriously involved with a man. Which I suspect is deliberate," she added.

There was some truth in what Nicole said, Shar had to admit. She loved her career as a real estate broker specializing in complicated trades. She met interesting people and got a great deal of satisfaction out of bringing off a difficult transaction. But it wasn't a nine-to-five job. She often worked evenings and weekends, often traveled out of the state, sometimes out of the country. But time alone wasn't what kept her from serious involvement with a male member of the human race. The truth was that her wariness toward men was more deeply rooted and longer lived than Nicole's recently acquired distrust...and it had been learned through painful experience. She had to concede, however, that the idea of deliberately testing a man on his ability to be faithful had never occurred to her.

Shar took another quick sip of wine. "Nikkie, in spite of what you may think about my talents as a—a temptress, this is way out of my line. And even if it weren't, I could never seriously consider doing what you're suggesting."

"Why not?" Nicole demanded.

"Because it's . . ." Shar shook her head a little helplessly. "Nikkie, how could you do this to the man you say you may be falling in love with? What if he found out? And on top of that, it wouldn't necessarily prove anything. If he resisted me and my amateurish attempt at seduction, it could just mean I'm not the type that appeals to him. A different woman could come along, and he'd follow like a panting puppy. And if he didn't resist me, that wouldn't prove anything, either. After all, the two of you aren't married or even engaged yet. If he could be lured away now, it doesn't mean he'd be tempted once he'd made a real commitment."

"If he could be lured away now, I don't want him," Nicole said with surprising vehemence. Shrewdly she added, "Would you?"

Shar didn't answer that question. She had already come to the rather unhappy conclusion that women were naturally monogamous. Men weren't.

"Why don't you just give the relationship more time?" Shar suggested. "You should be able to tell after a while if he's a man you can trust."

"Dave fooled me. Matt deceived you."

Shar sighed. "That's another one of the reasons that this test of yours really wouldn't prove anything. Dave was faithful for years and then just . . . went off the deep end. Maybe it can happen to anyone."

But Shar wondered now if Dave really had been faithful for years. What if someone had put him through a seduction test before the wedding ceremony? What if Matt had also had to take such a test? And her own father, as well? Maybe such a test ought to be required before marriage, like entrance exams before college.

Shar reached across the table and squeezed Nicole's hand. "Just give it some more time, okay?"

Nicole shook her head. "I can't. I think if I got out now, I could handle it. But if I keep seeing him, *really* fall in love and marry him, and then he . . ." Nicole turned her hand over and clutched Shar's fingers as if she were dangling over the edge of some bottomless precipice and those fingers were her lifeline. Her dark eyes were as vulnerable as those of a wild animal peering out of a trap. "He's attractive, Shar. *Very* attractive. There will always be women after him. I need to know . . . at least as much as I can know . . . about his inclination to be faithful. I need to know *now*."

Shar looked away. For a moment she had seen the same terror that had been in Nicole's eyes when she had come perilously close to complete emotional breakdown. Nicole was a sweet and wonderful person, warm and generous, the kind of woman who seemed to have been born to be a wife and mother. But she hadn't the inner strength, the steel backbone of someone less soft and fragile. Another betrayal like Dave's might really push her beyond her limit.

"Will you do it?" Nicole pressed.

"Even if I did say I'd do it—and I'm not saying I will, mind you," Shar emphasized, "I just don't see how we could carry it off."

"You can do it," Nicole assured her. With some of her old playfulness she added, "Just pretend you're trying to sell him on some big real estate deal. Only *you* are the prize offering in this transaction."

"I can't just waltz into his office and throw myself at him!" Shar protested. "And there's another thing. What about after the test is over? Am I going to have to stay in hiding the rest of my life? After doing something like what you're suggesting, my being around the two of you when you're married would be awkward, to say the least."

"I hadn't thought about that," Nicole admitted. "I want us all to be friends, of course, if Tal and I do marry."

"So do I. So let's think of something else, okay? Something a little more sane and sensible. And safer for both of us."

"What if he didn't know it was you?" Nicole speculated. She studied Shar's face and hair. "With a wig and makeup, a low-cut sexy gown instead of those conservative tailored suits you always wear—"

"No way." Shar's rejection was vehement. "No way am I going to go prancing around in some outrageous wig, with padding out to here." She made a gesture that extended her bustline to mammoth proportions.

Nicole gave that protest an airy brush-off. "You don't need any padding." Her dark eyes sparkled with all the old mischief of their days as college roommates. "What if *everyone* was in costume and wigs?"

"What do you mean?"

"Jim and Barbara Calvert are throwing a huge costume party to celebrate their tenth wedding anniversary next Saturday night. Tal and I are supposed to go. Jim and Barb throw terrific parties. It ought to be a lot of fun."

"And what do you have in mind?" Shar retorted. "That I'll crash the celebration and make off with Tal like some sort of female King Kong?"

Nicole giggled. In spite of her soft innocent sweetness, she had been the instigator of some very mischievous schemes back in college. "No, no . . . let me think."

Nicole tapped her narrow chin with a cinnamon-tipped fingernail, her eyes focused on an empty point in space just beyond Shar's left shoulder. Rapidly she came up with details.

"I'll arrange an invitation to the party for you. Then at the last minute I'll develop a migraine headache or something, and Tal will have to go alone."

"Why would he go alone?" Shar countered. "Somehow, from what you've told me, Tal doesn't sound like the kind of guy who'd be real thrilled by the prospect of a costume party to begin with. And if he really cares about you—even if he's just trying to convince you that he cares—he isn't going to go chasing off alone to a party while you're home sick.'"

"I suppose that's true," Nicole conceded. Then, undaunted, she tossed out an amended plan. "I'll think of some other reason I can't go to the party, something that won't arouse his sympathy, something that might even make him a little annoyed with me. I'll remind him that he has to go to the party because it's his chance to meet State Senator Stanford, who is a very powerful supporter of some upcoming state land-use legislation that may affect Tal's business. Lots of important contacts are made at these social events, you know."

Shar, frowning, twisted her wineglass back and forth between her slim fingers. It was a crazy idea, and yet in its own outrageous way it made a certain amount of sense. A costume party was the kind of event that fostered, under a cover of relative anonymity, excitement and recklessness. If ever a man was apt to stray, that would be the time he might do it. The results of such a "test" surely wouldn't be one hundred percent accurate, but they could indicate a man's reliability under pressure. Shar could see Nicole's point of view, unconventional as it might be.

Yet the idea of deliberately leading a man on made Shar's fingers tighten convulsively around the fragile glass. She knew Nicole thought of her as competent, self-assured and independent, capable of breezing through something like this. Shar had always been there for Nicole to lean on in times of crisis. She'd kept Nicole from packing up and running home during their first intimidating week of college. She'd been a bridesmaid when Nicole had married Dave, and Shar had offered her fiercely loyal support when the marriage had broken up a year ago.

But inside her polished career-woman shell, Shar knew she was neither as nonchalant nor as invulnerable as Nicole assumed. She had long ago learned to hide her hurt and disillusionment behind a barrier of self-reliance, but that didn't mean the vulnerability wasn't there.

And despite Shar's strength, her friendship with Nicole was in no way one-sided. A few years ago Nicole had opened both her heart and home to Shar when Shar's marriage had broken up under conditions not too different from Nicole's breakup. Nicole sent friends to Shar as clients and was always available to raise Shar's spirits with her gentle, sweetly generous and optimistic outlook on life . . . at least until Dave had knocked the props out from under her.

"Tal would never have to know it was you," Nicole was saying. "Please, Shar? I know it's a crazy idea. I know it's begging an awful lot of you. But I'm not asking you to actually go to bed with him to find out for certain if he's susceptible—"

"I should hope not!"

"Just . . . flirt with him. Get him into some situation where he thinks you're offering more than you really are, so you can tell whether he *would* make love to you. If he backs off, I'll know I have a man who can be trusted. If he doesn't back off, you can tell him to get lost. Or maybe you won't want to tell him to get lost. He's quite a guy, Shar. He really is. Maybe you'll want to grab him."

"No, thanks," Shar muttered. The last thing in the world she wanted was some attractive guy who had just proved he couldn't be faithful.

"I'll just need your shoulder to cry on for a while to get over the disappointment." Nicole's eyes were a little shiny, as if she was already anticipating tears.

"Nikkie, hon, just how far are you . . . uh . . . involved in this relationship?"

Nicole tilted her head, lips twitching impishly in a dramatic shift in mood. "If you want to know if I'm sleeping with him, why don't you just ask?"

"Okay, I'm asking."

"No, I'm not sleeping with him. He's made some advances, but he's never pressured me. I told him I needed time, and he seemed to understand."

Another point in Talcott O'Neal's favor, Shar conceded. "Do you want to make love with him?"

"I'm not sure," Nicole confessed. "There was never anyone but Dave, you know. I still feel a little strange just kissing another man. Mostly I think I'm afraid to get any more deeply involved until I know for certain what kind of man Tal really is. Will you help me?"

Still Shar hedged. "I really think you should give the guy the benefit of the doubt for a while."

"Just keep on walking around with my head in the clouds, thinking everything is fine, like I did with Dave—until it all crashes down around me. Is that what you're saying?" Bitterness hardened Nicole's usually gentle voice.

"No, not exactly—"

"Shar, this time I want to face reality *before* I get hit over the head with it."

A sensible enough precaution, Shar had to admit. Shar returned to methodically eating the food on her plate, the delicate flavor and creamy texture of the crab and mushroom casserole almost unnoticed now. Nicole removed the plates and brought coffee. She offered a luscious-looking chocolate mousse cake for dessert, which Shar declined.

In a way she had to admire Nicole for coming up with this idea, outrageous as it had seemed at first. At least Nicole was trying to not make the same mistake she'd made before, and it took a certain amount of stubborn courage to risk what she was doing. If only Shar herself didn't have to play such a starring role in the process!

"I'll take care of everything," Nicole went on, attacking the problems with the same dedication and enthusiasm with which she had planned the dinners that had helped

Dave move up the corporate ladder. "Let's see...what kind of costume should you wear? Tal and I were planning to go as Rhett Butler and Scarlett O'Hara from *Gone With the Wind*, although, as you guessed, Tal isn't really wild about this kind of thing."

Dismissing that, Nicole turned her attention to an appraisal of Shar. "I think you should be a harem girl," she decided. "A costume with lots of filmy gauze but that leaves your belly bare, a mysterious and sexy look. And a blond wig, of course. If Tal ever saw that real hair of yours, he'd be sure to recognize it when he saw it again."

Shar just sat there, letting Nicole make the decisions. This was one time, she suspected glumly, when blondes would not have more fun. She made one more effort to dissuade Nicole. "Tal sounds nice, Nikkie. I just don't think it's fair to try to entrap him, or whatever the legal word is."

"If Tal is the kind of man I want, he'll resist and he won't *be* entrapped," Nicole said firmly. "And I want you to put some real effort into this. Don't think you'll be doing me a favor by making a half-hearted pass at him and then assuring me that he's true blue. Turn on the high voltage. I know you can do it."

"And just where," Shar asked as an afterthought, "is the object of all this planning and scheming tonight?" It was, after all, Saturday night, an evening lovers-to-be usually spent together.

"He had to go down to the southern part of the state this weekend. Something about some property he still owns there."

She could always hope, Shar thought later, as she drove home to her apartment, that Nicole wouldn't be able to get her an invitation to the Calverts' anniversary party. An extra unattached woman usually wasn't high on the list of desirable additions to a party.

THAT HOPE EVAPORATED the following Monday when Nicole called the office and announced that everything was arranged. Shar was definitely invited. "Did you give them my real name?" Shar asked in dismay. There could be people at the party with whom she'd have to do business someday, so she certainly preferred to remain anonymous.

"No, I passed you off as my distant cousin from Los Angeles, with the name of Susan Provolt. You sell real estate to movie stars."

"Oh, very clever." Susan was Shar's middle name, Provolt the married name she'd discarded the minute she'd filed for divorce from Matt. It wasn't a name she was particularly fond of, but she wouldn't, at least, have any embarrassing problems remembering it. And if she was cornered, she did know a little about movie stars and southern California real estate. She had handled the Oregon end of a ranch trade for a rising macho-type star, one who had got a quick lesson in the fact that sexy fun and games with Shar didn't go with the deal.

Nicole went on to say that she had already arranged for Shar's costume and wig; they would be delivered the following Saturday morning, the day of the party. Nicole hadn't yet thought of a way to wriggle out of going to the party, but she was working on it. As a finishing touch, she was arranging for a limousine to transport Shar to the party.

This was a potent reminder that Nicole had a very different life-style from Shar's; Shar worked hard for her living. Although the women were best friends, it was a private friendship; they really didn't move in the same social circles. Dave had made excellent money as an executive with an insurance company—he still did—but it was Nicole's parents' status plus an inheritance from her grandparents that had provided luxuries and put Nicole and Dave into a higher-spending social set with the kind of people who threw big costume parties and hired limousines. Nor did Nicole have to work now that she was divorced, although Shar sometimes suspected Nicole would be better off if she had to get out and get a job. As it was, she puttered around the house and kitchen, still playing the role of housewife, even without a husband.

Could Talcott O'Neal have an eye on Nicole's money? Shar wondered. He'd apparently had plenty of money to buy out the failing modular-homes company, but appearances could be deceptive. This uneasy thought gave Shar the final nudge toward deciding to go through with the scheme.

Now that her mind was clear she could concentrate on her work. Her week was hectic, as usual. She had been back from southern California for three days but hadn't begun to catch up on all the work that had piled up during her absence. Of course, she hadn't expected to be away for six weeks. She'd gone down to the Los Angeles area on business, planning no more than a week's absence in which to take care of a three-way trade involving an apartment house and two office buildings. But she'd been felled by a fast-working virus, and after trying to keep working when she shouldn't have been, she had wound up briefly in the hospital. When she was released the doctor warned her to stay away from work or she'd have a relapse. Knowing that if she returned to Portland, work would track her down even if she tried to avoid it, she had stayed on with some friends in Ventura, spending a lot of time just loafing on the beach.

Now she was in fine shape physically, eager to dig into work with her usual energy. Numerous people had tried to contact her while she was away. She returned a few of the calls and got listings lined up on an office building, a resort lodge and a lakefront luxury home in the Lake Oswego area. All the owners were interested in trades as well as outright sales, and Shar was pleased that her reputation as a competent specialist in trades was evidently growing. She familiarized herself with the new listings on the office computer and attended the weekly conference with the other partners and the salespeople in the firm. She spent an entire day showing a fussy middle-aged couple an older apartment building. They wanted to see every nook and cranny, study every detail of the assumable financing, and Shar patiently went over everything with them. Her persistence paid off when they made a respectable offer that she was quite certain would be accepted by the sellers.

On Saturday morning Shar had to drive out to Lake Oswego to inspect the house she'd listed there, so she called the costume shop and arranged to pick up her harem outfit later in the day.

The trip took considerably longer than she'd expected, so she barely reached the costume shop before it closed. She rushed home, showered and, standing in lacy ice-blue bikini panties and bra, opened the carton.

She didn't know whether to be amused or shocked by what Nicole had chosen. When her friend made up her mind to test a man, she went all the way!

The costume probably bore no resemblance to any clothing worn in real life, past or present, but it was no cheap shoddy garment. The jade harem pants billowed sensuously around Shar's long legs. A sequined band caught the filmy material low on her hips, well below the navel. The tight-fitting sequined top ended just below her breasts and pushed the exposed upper curve into a ripe voluptuous swell. The back was a mere band across her bare skin, and she wound up having to remove her bra. The filmy sleeves were long but slit to gracefully flatter any movement of arms. The jeweled sandals had a rich barbaric look. There was a delicately tinted powder to give a golden glow to exposed skin, but Shar's toasted-gold skin hardly needed the extra coloring.

It was difficult to stuff her own lush tumble of hair under the blond wig, and she was surprised at how different the change in hair color made her look. She did her make-up with a more reckless hand than usual, boldly emphasizing her eyes with mascara and black eyeliner and smoky-plum eyeshadow. She added the glittery oversize jewels provided for forehead and navel before looking at herself again in the mirror.

Shar half gasped, half giggled. She was accustomed to being conservatively dressed for the office. Even on her occasional dates she generally maintained the aura of the competent businesswoman, making a subtle hands-off statement. This outfit looked anything *but* hands-off. It flaunted a sexiness that invited a caress at bare waist, a kiss in tempting cleavage; it promised sybaritic pleasures and pagan joys.

Shar stared at herself, uneasy with the transformation from competent real estate broker to temptress. What if she ran into someone she knew? On second thought, with a breathless little laugh she realized that wouldn't matter. She hardly recognized herself. And nonrecognition was the point of this masquerade, of course.

She tied the filmy jade veil across the lower half of her face, and the last of any worries that she might be recognized vanished. With that carefree feeling came another,

totally unexpected one, a recklessness born of her anonymity, a delightful flare of anticipation. She was someone else for tonight, someone flirty and teasing, daring and
reckless, with no need to worry about the consequences
of impetuous hot-blooded actions. Perhaps she'd meet an
exciting sheikh of her own tonight! Her eyes flashed green-
gold with excitement when she heard the limousine pull
up outside.

The telephone rang at the same moment; it was Nicole
with last-minute instructions. Tal had just left her house
for the party. She'd backed out at the last moment, saying
she'd heard her ex-husband might be there. They'd even
had a small quarrel about it, so if Tal had any tendency to
stray, this was surely a night when he would be susceptible to temptation. He was dressed Southern-gentleman
style: black river-boat-gambler suit, ruffled shirt, dashing phony mustache.

"He looks gorgeous," Nicole finished. She sighed. "I
must be crazy. I should just grab him and hold on tight instead of taking a risk like this."

"That's right. Why don't you get into your Scarlett
O'Hara outfit and—"

"Oh, no. You're not wriggling out of this so easily. How
do you look?"

"Like the poor little match girl wrapped in some gauze
curtains she found in the trash can."

Nicole just laughed. "You look gorgeous, and we both
know it. Is the limousine there yet?"

"Just arrived."

"Okay, well . . . good luck."

"In this instance, just exactly what does that mean?"

Another laugh, this one a little shaky. "I'm not sure.
But . . . thanks, Shar. There's not another friend in the
world who'd do something like this. You're one of a kind."

"Do you want a report tonight or in the morning?" Shar asked.

"Tonight! That is, unless you wind up spending the night with him. . . ."

Shar growled her opinion of that, grabbed a creamy cashmere evening shawl and hurried out to the waiting limousine.

2

SHAR WAS FAMILIAR with the Calverts' house; she had been through it a couple of years ago when it had been on the market. Now, as then, its vaguely Southern-plantation style, the tall white columns and curved steps, struck her as out of place and pretentious in the Northwest. No doubt the perfect house for a costume party for a couple hundred "close friends," she thought wryly.

Shar had no particular game plan in mind for the evening, but it occurred to her as the limousine pulled into the circular driveway that Talcott O'Neal, even if he was susceptible to temptation, wasn't apt to try anything too incriminating at the party. She needed to be free for after-party possibilities. With that thought in mind she told the chauffeur she wouldn't be needing him anymore that evening. *Just listen to me*, she thought, almost giggling as the driver nodded deferentially. *Dismissing the chauffeur and playing the grand lady as if I'd been born to it.* If the evening didn't have such a deadly serious purpose, she could have almost enjoyed the novelty of all this. If Tal didn't prove susceptible, and she fervently hoped he wouldn't, she'd call a taxi later.

The cool damp air of an Oregon winter chilled Shar's bare midriff as she dashed up the broad steps. *How attractive*, she speculated lightly, *is a harem girl with goose bumps?* Light from tall windows spilled onto the sloping lawn, and the grass gleamed wetly from an earlier rain.

Shar was a little late; music met her as the elaborate double doors opened.

A maid took Shar's shawl, leaving her feeling uncomfortably exposed in the gauzy, midriff-bared outfit. She clutched protectively at the only thing she had left to clutch, her little gold-mesh evening bag. Her earlier moment of reckless excitement had drained away, leaving her wondering what on earth had possessed her to get involved in this incredible scheme.

She knew the answer to that, of course. Nicole. She had only to remember how Dave's betrayal had devastated Nicole, how it had also confused and hurt little Cindy, to feel a revival of protective concern. If Nicole believed she had to know if Tal could be trusted, Shar was determined to help her.

She decided the first order of business was to offer obligatory congratulations to the host and hostess. If she only knew who they were . . .

Then she spied what had to be the happy couple: a glowing woman in a white bridal gown that was stretched to cover her figure, which was apparently somewhat heavier than it had been, and a ruddy-faced, slightly embarrassed-looking man in a formal tuxedo. Shar wound her way through the crowd, accepting a drink along the way, more for holding purposes than anything else. She signed the guest book, murmured her congratulations and in return got a gushy "You look *fantastic*, we'll have to get together soon." Shar just smiled and nodded, refraining from pointing out that they'd never met.

That duty done, Shar wandered around, trying to spot Talcott O'Neal. Most of the guests had gone in more for glamour than humor with their costumes. She saw one long-eared rabbit and a robot, but there were several can-can girls, Civil War heroines and movie star look-alikes.

And a plenitude of harem girls, she realized a little ruefully, in costumes not unlike her own.

Surprisingly, that suddenly made her feel more comfortable than awkward, more safely anonymous. Some of
her earlier adventurous spirit returned, and she took a sip
of her drink. *Here I am, a seductive female on the prowl,
so you guys had better watch out.* As the stemmed glass
got tangled in her veil, Shar tried not to contradict her
practiced sultry glance with a giggle.

How come she felt giggly? A professional, competent
real estate broker should not feel adventurous and bubbly and giggly. But tonight she wasn't an efficient serious-
minded businesswoman. Tonight she was someone else,
someone flirty and reckless, someone who walked with a
sultry swing of her hips and a toss of her platinum hair,
someone who boldly fluttered her mascara-laden lashes
at strangers.

She wandered into another room, where several people
were dancing to music from a gaudy old-fashioned juke-
box. Others were playing pool under a Tiffany lamp. She
peered beyond that into a hot-tub room—which hadn't
been there before, she recalled—and shook her head at a
friendly invitation to join the exuberant participants in the
bubbling water.

Still no sight of anyone who matched Nicole's description of Talcott O'Neal. However, she felt other interested
eyes occasionally following her. Shar seriously doubted
that the man was as attractive as Nicole had described
him. Uneasily she suspected that when she found him, he
would bear a disconcerting resemblance to Nicole's former husband. Love might not be blind, she sighed, but
sometimes it wore distorting lenses. Wouldn't it be funny
if she wandered around all evening and never found him?
What if he hadn't come, after all? That, she decided, would

be the best recommendation she could think of for the man.

Then she saw him. He was standing beside the enormous white fireplace in the living room, one foot casually braced on the raised hearth. It had to be him—dashingly cut black suit, ruffled white shirt, dark hair, devil-be-damned mustache, dazzling smile. Shar wasn't certain the clothing accurately represented either Rhett Butler or Civil War times, but this man certainly projected the virile recklessness of that fictional hero. He had an electric vitality, a potent male forcefulness that rocketed halfway across the room and hit Shar somewhere in the middle of her jeweled navel.

But it was just a fictional projection, she reminded herself, trying to shake off that first moment of explosive impact. This was a costume party. In real life Tal O'Neal was probably just an ordinary construction firm owner, no more like this sexy dashing figure than she was like her own flirty harem-girl persona.

Yet except for the mustache, which she knew wasn't real, Tal wasn't all that much in costume. The dark good looks, the brilliant smile, rugged frame and dark curly hair were his own. And that forceful, almost shocking aura of virility had nothing to do with his costume or his phony mustache. Was this the man who had been understanding when Nicole had held back on an intimate physical relationship, Shar wondered doubtfully. If so, although he exuded virile impatience, perhaps his patience with Nicole proved that he really was in love with her.

Though, based on Nicole's description, he could be mistaken for Nicole's former husband, in the flesh there was little resemblance. He looked at ease, self-assured, fully capable of handling men on a rough construction site—or a woman in his arms.

And he had a small entourage of females around him, Shar realized as she shook herself out of her stupor. He didn't appear to be suffering from acute loneliness because Nicole hadn't come along. If she wanted to seduce Talcott O'Neal, Shar thought grimly, it appeared she would have to stand in line.

She moved around behind the piano, the better to study him while keeping herself out of sight. By now, after making some discreet inquiries at the office and among some business friends about O'Neal Construction, Shar knew a little more about the man. He had a reputation in southern Oregon for being hard driving, reliable, thoroughly capable. And ruthless when it came to dealing with incompetence or disloyalty. In his personal life he was apparently something of a loner. He had entered the Portland construction scene aggressively and already had a contract to supply modular buildings for a new apartment complex in one of the suburbs.

Nicole of course, Shar remembered with a smile, hadn't even known what modular construction was. Nor had she been terribly interested when Shar had explained that it meant a building was factory constructed in two or more complete units, trucked to the site, then assembled on a previously prepared foundation.

Tal evidently appreciated Nicole for what she was, a charming hostess, a good mother—a domestic woman who would happily devote herself to being a man's wife, leaving the details of business to him. Which, as Nicole herself feared, didn't insure that Tal couldn't be tempted by some alluring little sexpot. Suddenly Shar realized that Tal was moving away from the trio of admiring females, expertly extricating himself with some smiling excuse. She didn't stop to think where he might be going. She saw this as her chance and boldly snatched it. She stepped out from behind the piano, directly into his path.

But just as swiftly, a more basic shyness, a reluctance made her pull back. By then it was too late to avoid collision. Bodies crashed together, and Shar's barely touched drink spilled an icy cascade down her bare middle, which certainly wasn't what she had planned.

Lesson number one, she thought as she looked in dismay at the rivulets trailing across her bare skin. *If you're going to bump into a man, have the good sense to get rid of your crushed ice first.*

"Hey, I'm sorry!" His strong, slightly rough hands caught her shoulders and kept her from tumbling backward. "I didn't mean to run over you." His fingers slid inside the slits in her sleeves and rested on bare skin. They felt strong and competent.

"I...uh...guess I spilled my drink." Great opening line. Shar groaned to herself. Really fascinating. What man could resist? Her great seduction scene was starting out more like a Three Stooges comedy.

"Are you all right?"

Shar looked up into his eyes. "Gorgeous green brown," Nicole had described them, but she hadn't done them justice. Their impact went far beyond mere color. Yet whatever earthy delights they promised were not for Shar; the look he focused on her was one of polite concern.

"Just a little damp," she finally assured him.

He produced a clean white handkerchief and with no apparent self-consciousness started dabbing at the splatters of liquid and ice at her bare waist. Shar held her stomach muscles taut, scarcely breathing, partly in response to the icy dousing, partly in reaction to the touch of his hands. He was holding her waist with his left hand to steady her while he bent over and soaked up the liquid with the handkerchief in his other hand. The light grip of his fingers felt unreasonably warm. She had a close-up of his crisp curly hair. It had the fresh-washed fragrance of some outdoorsy-scented masculine shampoo. Nice hair for a woman to run her fingers through, she thought irrelevantly. Nice nape of neck for a kiss. . . .

He straightened and pocketed the handkerchief. "You probably ought to try to wash the drink out of your costume. It may stain."

"Yes, I'll do that."

He was looking over her head now, searching the colorful crowd for someone. He obviously wasn't planning to hang around to see if she might spill something on *him* next. Nor, she realized, did he appear interested in taking advantage of the situation by rushing her off to some dark corner and playing touch and feel games under the guise of helping to remove the stain. So far, though, she hadn't shown him that she was interested in anything more than polite chatter. He seemed on the point of walking away, and she searched her mind for something seductive and intriguing to say. Whatever had made Nicole think Shar could turn on the "high voltage"? Her mind was as empty of suggestive small talk as a blank cassette.

"Have you seen the hot tub?" she finally managed to blurt out. "It looks like fun. . . . I wonder if swimsuits are required?"

"They probably have extras for guests if you didn't bring one." His tone was polite.

She summoned up a flirtatious flutter of her eyelashes. "I meant . . . skinny-dipping would be a lot more fun, don't you think?"

"I'm afraid I don't go in for . . . ah . . . group activities of that sort." He looked a little uncomfortable and wary, as if he thought she might do something embarrassing right there on the spot.

"Perhaps we could manage a twosome instead." She smiled invitingly, then remembered that the veil hid her mouth. She reached out and pretended to straighten a ruffle on his shirt, letting her fingers linger on his chest and then glide up to caress his jaw. "I'm here alone, and it's such a big crowd...."

"Thanks, but I'm not planning to stay long." He ran a finger across the phony mustache, frowning as if he were half inclined to rip it off. "This mob scene really isn't my favorite kind of social gathering."

"Perhaps we could think of something more interesting and private to do together." That ought to be blunt enough. Just then, she was doubly grateful for the anonymity the veil and costume gave her. She'd never have been able to say any of these things without them. Beneath the veil she felt a glow of embarrassment hot enough to set the filmy material on fire.

"I don't think so. I have some plans." Again his gaze roamed the room.

"Are you looking for someone?" she asked. She tilted her head to give him a deliberately coquettish glance over the veil. "Not a wife, I hope." Meaningfully she added, "At least not a wife here tonight, I hope."

He laughed, as if he suddenly found her blatant flirtation more amusing than tempting. His eyes played over her, skimming the exposed upper swell of breasts and trim midriff, outlining the silhouette of long legs beneath the filmy harem pants. Shar couldn't tell what his reaction was. His eyes were unrevealing. Which, she reflected, *was* a meaningful reaction. The right reaction. And he hadn't bothered to acknowledge her suggestive comments about a wife.

"Actually I was on my way to try to have a word with Senator Stanford. But I don't see him now."

Shar glanced around and spotted the portly member of the state legislature generously helping himself to hors d'oeuvres and beaming at the pretty girl holding the tray. He had a reputation as something of a ladies' man. "Isn't that the senator over there?"

Tal's gaze followed the nod of Shar's head toward the man in the George Washington costume. "Doesn't look as if he'd be too interested in discussing land-use planning at the moment, does it?" Tal commented wryly.

Shar hesitated, and then her adventurous spirit took over . . . or perhaps what she was feeling was simple relief. Tal had passed the test with flying colors. He'd been polite and good-humored about the collision, but nothing more. Nor had he exhibited any real interest in the female admirers who had collected around him at the fireplace; he had walked off and left them. He had come here hoping to meet the senator, and apparently that was all he was interested in. The test hadn't really become as intimate as Nicole had suggested, but as far as Shar was concerned it had gone far enough. She had a pleasantly bubbly feeling of freedom. She'd tried, and that was that. Her duty was done. There was no point in carrying this ridiculous test farther. And Talcott O'Neal deserved a reward for resisting temptation, amateurish though her efforts might have been.

"Let me introduce you to the senator," she said gaily.

"You know him?"

No, as a matter of fact, Shar didn't know Senator Stanford except by reputation. But she didn't let that stop her. She gained boldness from her effervescent feeling that her duty was now over. She led the way to where the senator was still engaging the pretty girl in conversation and touched him on the shoulder. He turned, his pale blue eyes brightening when he saw yet another pretty girl.

"Senator Stanford, how nice to see you again! Isn't this a terrific party? You look absolutely fabulous in that costume. I hope I detect presidential leanings in your future?"

"Well, one never knows." He beamed with pleasure at her gushy praise.

She turned and brought Tal forward with a touch on his arm. "Oh, Senator Stanford, I'd like to introduce someone who is most interested in your new legislation on land-use planning. This is Ta—" The name was almost out before Shar remembered that she wasn't supposed to know who he was. She glanced at Tal, wondering if he'd caught the near slip.

Apparently not. "Tal O'Neal, O'Neal Construction," he filled in. He extended a hand toward the older man. "I've been wanting to meet you ever since I moved my construction business up from the Medford area."

Shar discreetly faded away, suspecting she was missed more by the senator with an eye for the ladies then by Tal. Actually she ought to feel a bit miffed. Tal had treated her with the same polite consideration he might have given a little old lady who needed help crossing the street. Attractive men usually reacted more positively to her than *that*. Nicole really had found herself a prize.

She glanced back and saw that the two men were already deep in conversation. Shar was too fond of her best friend to feel envy, but she couldn't escape a certain wistfulness that such a man had never come into her life. Vitally attractive, ambitious, considerate, interesting. And faithful. That was the quality Shar knew she valued above all else in a man. She'd had too much experience with the other kind.

She found a powder room and used the dampened corner of a towel to sponge the remains of the drink out of her costume, then pressed the damp spot between two towels. After exchanging a few isn't-this-a-great-party comments with a cancan girl and a Marilyn Monroe lookalike, she glanced at her watch, hidden beneath the sequined band at her wrist. She hadn't eaten dinner. There was supposed to be a buffet meal later, but she really didn't feel like staying for it. Nicole, she knew, enjoyed this type of large-scale social event, but Shar wasn't particularly fond of them.

She found a maid and picked up her shawl. It was a little rude to leave so early, so she took a leisurely and rather circuitous route to the door. A man in a vaudeville-style straw hat and a garter armband was playing the piano and she paused, enjoying the lively music.

She had just remembered that she couldn't simply leave, that she must call a taxi first—when she felt a touch on her elbow.

"I was looking for you," Tal said. "You disappeared before I had a chance to thank you for introducing me to Senator Stanford."

"You really didn't need an introduction. I'm sure that at this kind of party you could have introduced yourself."

"That's true, I suppose." He smiled. "But with a man like the senator, I'm sure the . . . uh . . . sponsorship of an attractive woman never hurts. Anyway, thanks."

He flashed that smile again, and Shar had the peculiar feeling that a light had just come on in a dark room. Which was foolishness, of course. This room was well lighted and lively. But sometimes there was a darkness inside her. . . .

"By the way," he added, "the senator said your name had slipped his mind, and I couldn't supply it for him, of course."

"Actually I don't even know the senator."

"You mean you just . . . ?"

"Faked it," Shar filled in with a guilty smile.

Tal laughed, genuine husky laughter, not that faintly derogatory chuckle with which he'd greeted her earlier attempts at flirtation. It was a pleasant sound, one a woman could easily become addicted to. "Why?" he asked curiously. Evidently her audacity didn't displease him.

She couldn't explain the real reason, of course, that she had felt Tal deserved a little reward for his exemplary behavior. "Just an…impulse of the moment, I guess. I didn't mean any harm."

"I'm sure you gave the senator's spirits a lift—and kept the rusty gears in his mind whirring as he tried to remember who you were. I understand he's something of a ladies' man, so he'll probably come looking for you to renew the acquaintance."

Great. Just what she needed. A lecherous old politician chasing after her. If she hadn't already made the decision to leave, she would have then. "Well, if you see him, tell him I've gone. Tell him my sheikh called me back to the harem or something."

"And what name shall I *not* tell him?"

Shar hesitated momentarily, not because she couldn't remember the name, but because it would be the first outright lie she'd told while perpetrating this little scheme, and it didn't come easily to her. She also felt a moment of uneasiness about why Tal wanted to know. "Susan Provolt."

He noticed the cashmere shawl draped over her arm. "Are you actually leaving?"

"If the senator is looking for me, I think I'd better." Shar laughed. "I hope your discussion with him proved worthwhile. Most people seem to feel the senator's bill will be extremely detrimental to economic development in the state. If you'll excuse me?" She glanced around, looking for a phone.

"Did you bring a car?"

"I was just looking for a telephone so I could call a taxi."

They had by now gradually drifted away from the piano. Tal was looking at her with an undecided expression, eyes suddenly a little more guarded than they had been only moments earlier. Shar remembered now that he'd also made a comment about leaving the party early. Was he considering offering her a ride? And if he was, was it innocent repayment for her small favor...or something else?

She had a sudden dismaying surge of doubt. Had she been premature in granting Tal a passing grade? Was he the kind of man who put business first but, when business was over, was ready and willing to play the kind of sexy games she had hinted at?

What she wanted to do was give him the benefit of the doubt, as she had advised Nicole to do. She was extremely reluctant to step back into this shady scheme. But the memory of Nicole's fervent request that she use some high voltage in her seduction efforts kept her from simply walking away. Giving Tal high marks for being faithful and trustworthy if he really wasn't would be the worst thing she could do for Nicole, because Nicole would then walk into the relationship with a trusting heart, wide open to calamity.

Unwillingly Shar asked, "You wouldn't care to give a stranded lady a lift, would you?" Again she attempted to bat her eyelashes, although she doubted that the unenthusiastic gesture could be described as "high voltage."

"I suppose I could." Still he hesitated, not actually making the offer.

"Don't let me inconvenience you. I believe you mentioned some other plans . . . ?"

What kind of plans? Shar wondered now. Going back and making up the small quarrel with Nicole? Or did he have something exciting going on the side that Nicole didn't know about?

Damn him, she thought, suddenly angry. She'd been so *sure* about him for a few minutes. She flung the shawl savagely around her shoulders.

"I'd be happy to give you a ride. It's the least I can do to repay you for your help . . . and to aid you in escaping the senator's clutches." She looked up to see an appealingly conspiratorial twinkle in his eyes.

Shar swallowed, feeling as if she had somehow slipped back into a trap after believing she was free. Yet at the same time it was an almost treacherously inviting trap. The invitation was *nice*, not suggestive. "Do you want to say a word to the hostess before we leave?" she asked.

Tal turned to look at the plump bride who was mingling regally with her guests. "Actually I don't even know the couple. They're friends of a . . . friend."

A friend. Nicole. Was that the way a man identified a woman he was in love with? It probably was if he was planning a little extracurricular activity, Shar thought resentfully. She couldn't keep her feelings about this man on an even keel. One moment he seemed a prince of reliability, the next a devil of danger.

"How about you?" he asked.

"I don't know them, either."

His short laugh was a little wry. "If I ever get to a tenth wedding anniversary, this damn sure isn't the way I intend to spend it."

"How would you spend it?"

"Intimate dinner for two. Candlelight. Flowers. Dancing. Walking hand in hand under the stars." He suddenly looked a little embarrassed, as if he'd revealed a romantic nature he usually kept hidden. "Anyway, I think we're free to leave without expressing our regrets to the host and hostess. They'll never miss us."

Casually, a little like two children sneaking out of school to play hooky, they worked their way to the door and made their escape. Outside, a downpour greeted them.

"You wait here. I'll bring the car around."

Shar was about to protest. She wouldn't have minded a dash through the rain. But it occurred to her that a harem girl wrapped in wet gauze was hardly seductive. She nodded and wrapped the shawl a little more tightly around her shoulders as she waited.

The car, something small and sporty and foreign made that Shar couldn't identify in the heavy rain, pulled into the circular driveway a few moments later. Shar dashed out and slid into the car.

"Good old Oregon weather, isn't it?" Tal commented.

"Oregonians don't tan, they rust, remember?" Shar said, quoting a popular bumper sticker.

"You're tanned," he commented with a brief sideways glance as he nosed the car into the wet street. The rain blocked the probe of headlights like a silvery wall.

The fact that she was tanned was something he must have noted earlier, because inside the car there was only a faint glow from the dashboard lights. The wall of pouring rain outside made the small interior feel unexpectedly intimate. It wasn't, Shar reflected, what she thought of as a family man's car.

"And you," she said with accusing playfulness, "no longer have that devastatingly attractive mustache."

"Sure I do." He patted his jacket pocket. "It's just that it's in my pocket instead of on my upper lip."

They laughed together. Shar wished she could as easily rid herself of the wig. It was beginning to feel itchy.

"Recent refugee from California?" he prodded, not forgetting that she hadn't responded to his comment about the tan.

"No." Shar didn't elaborate. She might be trying to seduce this man, but she had no intention of giving him any revealing personal information. Then the thought occurred to her that she could tell him any frivolous story she cared to invent; she wasn't obliged to stick with facts. What kind of "facts" would be apt to intrigue Talcott O'Neal? If he was out for a quick fling, perhaps a fact that she was here only temporarily and not averse to a one-night romp without complications or commitments?

"I'm here visiting my elderly aunt. Her idea of a high old time is putting a tablespoon of Scotch in her coffee. I thought it would be nice to get out and meet some of these lusty Northwest loggers and cowboys I've heard about." This invention didn't feel so much like a lie as it did making up an interesting story, as she did for Cindy when the little girl stayed overnight with her. "I hear they're very...mmm...virile."

"Then how come you left the party?" he asked. "I saw some rather lusty glances thrown your way. I'm sure there were plenty of opportunities there."

"I did make the effort," Shar said ingeniously. "But you didn't seem interested. And you were the only man there who...appealed to me."

"I'm flattered." His tone was unexpectedly dry. "Where did you want me to drop you off?"

Shar gave him the address, not thinking until after she did so that at some later date this could cause complications. Would Tal make some connection between Nicole's best friend, Shar Hathaway, and a certain amorous blonde named Susan Provolt living at the same address? Probably not, she concluded. If Tal and Nicole married, she would probably see Nicole as she had when Nicole was married to Dave, mostly on a women-only basis.

"You're not going to take me home without even offering me a drink, are you?" she asked, injecting a pouty note into her voice. "It's early yet."

"I thought the 'it's early yet' line belonged to the man on the prowl."

"Feminism. Men aren't the only ones who prowl these days. Aren't you into feminism?"

"Are you asking for a philosophical discussion?" he inquired.

"Not really."

"I didn't think so."

He headed in the general direction of her apartment, evidently fairly familiar with the city in spite of not having lived there long. She had to point out the last couple of turns, after which she indicated the private house in which she had a second-story apartment. Actually she owned the house and rented out the main portion of it. Making an excellent buy was an occasional advantage of being in the real estate business.

"Well, thanks for bringing me home." What now? "And saving me from the senator."

"You know, I haven't figured out what your game is, but I don't believe a word of that little story about your visiting an elderly aunt." He spoke casually, more conversationally than accusingly.

"You don't?" Shar didn't know what to say. She thought she'd sounded quite convincing. She laughed a little weakly. "I'm a married woman out on the town while my husband is away?"

"Nope. I looked at your left hand. No ring. No white line where a ring usually is." So what was he doing checking out things like that if he was so trustworthy, Shar wondered suspiciously.

"The fact is . . ." Shar took a deep breath while her mind raced to invent something plausible. "I'm doing research for a first-hand report on how hard it is for a woman to meet attractive men."

"I doubt that you have any problems along those lines."

"Why not?" Shar demanded, a little indignant that he had instantly rejected what she considered a rather clever ploy.

Without speaking he deliberately dropped his eyes to the luminous swell of skin exposed above the tight sequined top of the harem outfit. The insinuation was that she had too much seductive equipment going for her to make meeting men difficult. Her inclination was to yank the shawl around her, but she forced herself to leave it open and lean toward him suggestively.

"But I don't appeal to *you*?" she asked with husky meaning.

"You . . . puzzle me." His gaze was openly speculative.

It was also, she thought, an open door for some further invitation from her. To ask him to come up to her apartment? No way. She had agreed to this outlandish scheme, but there was a limit to how far she was willing to carry it. She had no intention of being trapped in her apartment with a man who suddenly wouldn't take no for an answer. Tal wasn't some nervous schoolboy to be tested and graded and dismissed.

But simply inviting him inside didn't mean she had to actually allow him in, she reminded herself. A yes answer from him would definitely tip the scales toward a failing grade, and she could still back out.

Which was probably what she was going to have to do, she thought as he continued to look at her speculatively across the gap between the luxurious bucket seats.

"Then perhaps you should come inside so we can get better acquainted." She threw everything she had into that one line, abandoning the flutter of eyelashes to which he seemed impervious, uttering the words with throaty promise. She swallowed, glad the veil was there to conceal the nervous throat spasm that followed the invitation. "*Much* better acquainted."

"No thanks."

Shar tried not to let her relief show, but still she persisted. "Another time?"

"No, thanks."

No explanation, no excuses. Shar liked that. It was a peculiar feeling, she thought, coming on to a man and then liking him because he politely but flatly rejected her.

"Well, thanks for the ride then." She opened the door and slid out of the car. She walked to the side stairs that led up to the outside entrance of her apartment. When she looked back the car was still there. Why, she wondered uneasily. She peered out the window as soon as she stepped inside the dark apartment, just in time to see the departing taillights. He had waited to see that she was safely inside, she realized. He wasn't tempted by what she had fairly blatantly offered him, but he was concerned enough about her as a person to make certain that she was inside before he left.

A nice man, she thought, relief and regret mingling with some other emotions she couldn't identify at the moment. A good man. Faithful. Dependable. And very, very attractive. Maybe he had a brother, she thought, smiling tremulously in the dark. She'd have to ask Nicole.

At the thought of Nicole, Shar switched on a light and hurried to the telephone. It was possible that Tal was headed for Nicole's house right now, and she wanted to call with the favorable report before he got there. This could be the night they'd make up . . . and make love for the first time. Shar shoved away an inexplicable and unwanted pang at that thought and dialed Nicole's number.

Nicole answered on the first ring. Shar gave her a light-hearted report and emphasized Tal's absolute and total resistance to temptation.

"You really tried?" Nicole demanded.

"I came on like gangbusters," Shar assured her. "He resisted not just once but twice. The man is invulnerable. Solid and dependable as a chunk of granite. He gave me a ride home out of pure gentlemanly politeness when I coerced him into it, but he was having nothing to do with any invitation to come inside."

Shar could hear Nicole's wobbly release of breath as she accepted the verdict. "Thanks, Shar. I can't begin to thank you enough. Now I feel that I can . . . love him without being afraid I'm falling into some quicksand trap."

"Invite me to the wedding."

"You're a bridesmaid, of course. You're a bridesmaid at all my weddings," Nicole added with a return of her occasionally impish sparkle.

"He doesn't happen to have a brother, does he?"

"Not that I know of. Why?"

"Oh, just checking. He's quite a guy, Nikkie. He really is. Hang on to him."

"I will. And Shar . . ."

"Yes?"

"Someday a guy will come along for you, too. Don't be bitter about all men. There are a few good ones out there."

Shar gave an unladylike snort. Then they both laughed and said good-night.

Shar intended to put all thoughts of the evening out of her mind and file it away as a mildly incredible experience, one she didn't care to repeat. Friendship or no, if Tal didn't work out, Nicole was going to have to find someone else to run her seduction tests.

Yet bits and pieces of the evening kept drifting back into Shar's thoughts. Tal's husky honest laughter. His small revelation of a hidden sweetly romantic nature. The fun feeling of conspiracy as they had sneaked out of the party together. His firm "No, thanks" to her final invitation. An impression that he had depths of character that went beyond anything she had tested. That potent aura of leashed sexual power, all the more potent because she knew he hadn't been making any effort to project it. If he ever chose to turn on his full seductive power... Shar left that thought unfinished and unexplored. It was too dangerous.

On Sunday afternoon she took an older, out-of-town couple around to see several modest houses. They were interested in trading their rural home for something of equal or lesser value, so that they wouldn't have to put out much cash or go into debt. She was sorry that nothing seemed really suitable for them.

Monday went better. She returned the costume, glad to be rid of it. A deal that had been hanging fire since before she went to Los Angeles suddenly went through. She took some papers to the title company and had just returned to the office when the receptionist motioned to her.

"Call for you, Shar. I was just about to tell him you weren't in. Line one."

"Thanks, Lil. I'll take it in my office." Shar paused long enough to throw her raincoat across a chair—wasn't it *ever* going to stop raining?—then picked up the phone. "Shar Hathaway speaking. May I help you?"

"This is Tal O'Neal."

3

SHAR EXPERIENCED a very unbusinesslike jolt at the husky sound of his voice. She knew she'd have recognized it even if he hadn't identified himself. Then panic billowed through her. Why was he calling her? How had he found out her real identity?

Anger supplanted the panic. He'd no doubt gone back to Nicole Saturday night, and now he was calling *her*?

"Yes?" Crystals of frost edged the word.

"I have some industrial property down in the southern part of the state. I've been trying to sell it but not having much luck. Someone gave me your name as someone who is extremely capable at setting up trades."

The anger and panic drained away in a flash flood of relief. This call had no connection with Saturday night; it was strictly business. He had no idea she was the flirty-eyed blonde who had invited him to her apartment. She suddenly felt guilty for even her brief suspicion; he had proven himself to be totally trustworthy. Yet at the same time she was distinctly reluctant to get involved in any business dealings with him. Why? Because of Nicole and that entire ridiculous test? Or because she was afraid that—

"Are you there?"

"Yes. I—I was just reaching for my scratch pad." Snatching up the pad, she poised a pen over it to make the statement true. There was no point in turning away a potentially valuable client. He obviously didn't recognize her voice. Maybe Nicole had given Tal her name, trying to do her a business favor in return for her help.

"Do you happen to remember who gave you my name?" she asked cautiously.

"No . . . someone at a Homebuilders' Association meeting, I think." He sounded a little impatient, as if the question was irrelevant. Which it was.

Briskly she asked, "What type of property would you be interested in trading for?"

"What I really need is some heavy equipment. My previous construction work didn't require a crane, but I need one to handle the modular units. I've been hiring a crane from another company, but that isn't practical on a long-term basis. Did I mention that I'm the owner of O'Neal Construction? I took over the old Madrona Modular Homes plant. Unfortunately their crane was repossessed before I got the company.

Shar realized she was going to have to be careful in dealing with Tal. She already knew most of this. It would be all too easy to slip, arousing his curiosity by revealing how much she did know about him—personally as well as professionally.

"But I don't suppose you have any dealings with heavy equipment," he added.

"No, not directly. However, we have a listing on which the owners just recently indicated a willingness to consider a trade, and they mentioned an interest in southern Oregon property. If you'll hold on a moment, I'll check." Shar cradled the phone on her shoulder and keyed information into the computer to bring up the listing she had in mind. "Yes, here it is—"

"That was quick."

"The marvels of the computer age. Also a nice excuse when things go wrong, because we can always blame it on the computer."

He laughed and the pleasant sound sent sparks dancing through her. "I'll have to consider getting one for my office, especially for inventory. Someone is always running in to tell me we just ran out of some minor little necessity—like boards or nails."

Shar determinedly ignored the irrelevant sparks. "I don't know if this would interest you or not. This listing is for some warehouse property in the industrial area. Several pieces of equipment, including a crane, go with it."

"I don't know that I'd be interested in that particular type of property, but I might keep the equipment and turn around and resell the property itself. I'd be interested in taking a look at it, anyway. And I do want to list my property with you."

Shar went on to ask him about his southern Oregon property and jotted down such details as description and price. She'd have Lil type them into a listing for him to sign later. Conscientiously she reminded him that trades often had different federal and state income tax consequences from outright sales and he should discuss this with his accountant before making any decisions.

"Thanks. I appreciate that."

He sounded a little surprised, as if he hadn't expected that type of honest cautionary information. For her part Shar was impressed that he apparently hadn't given a second thought to dealing with a woman real estate broker in this type of case. Occasionally she encountered clients who patronized women with the attitude that they were okay for selling houses but were surely too fluff-headed to handle big investments in commercial and industrial property.

"May I look at the property and equipment sometime tomorrow afternoon?"

Shar glanced down in dismay at her jotted notes. The end of the ballpoint pen had a peculiar wiggle; her hand was trembling. Perhaps she could get Ron Howland to take him out there— No, Ron was tied up trying to settle a dispute between the buyers and sellers of a small office building—before the matter wound up in court. Besides, trades were her responsibility in this office. She mustn't let personal matters interfere with business.

"Yes, that will be fine." They settled on a time for him to come to her office, and Shar briskly wound up the conversation. "Thank you for contacting me, Mr. O'Neal. We'll do our best to arrange a suitable trade or sale for you."

Shar fingered the ballpoint pen nervously after hanging up the phone. There was no reason to feel uneasy about this. She was reasonably certain that her identity was safe and equally certain that Nicole would have no objections to her doing business with Tal. Still, she decided to call and discuss this development with Nicole just to be positive.

She immediately dialed Nicole's number, but the woman who occasionally took care of Cindy was there. Nicole was having her hair done. No doubt for a date with Tal, Shar surmised.

Shar had to show a small apartment building at five-thirty, and by the time she got to her own apartment and tried to call again, Nicole had already gone out.

The following morning Shar ran out to Lake Oswego, then met a client for a late lunch, and by the time she got back to the office, Tal was just getting out of a pickup in the parking lot.

Shar started to call out a greeting to him but clamped her jaw shut before the incriminating words could escape. She wasn't supposed to know who he was. Today he was dressed in rough work clothes, as if he had just come from a construction site: tan cords, translucent raincoat, heavy boots. He wasn't Rhett Butler today, but he lacked nothing of that masculine flare and dash. He had probably been wearing a hard hat at the construction site, but now he was hatless, and the relentless rain beaded his dark hair with glistening droplets as soon as he was out of the pickup.

They reached the main entrance at the same time, and he moved to open the door for her. Some women might scorn gestures like that, but Shar still liked them. She smiled, careful not to give away that she knew who he was. "Thank you."

"Are you by any chance Miss Hathaway?" he asked. Raindrops glittered like jewels tucked into his heavy eyebrows.

"Shar Hathaway, yes."

"I'm Tal O'Neal. We had an appointment . . . ?"

"Yes, of course. I'm so pleased to meet you." They were inside the carpeted office by then, and she offered him a businesslike handshake. "Lil typed up the listing on your property. Perhaps you'd like to look it over and give her some additional information that we need."

He was watching her with a faintly puzzled expression on his face, a small frown line between the dark arches of his brows. Did her in-person voice jangle something in his memory? His green-brown eyes appraised her in a way that made her feel he could see into the darkest corners of her mind.

But he couldn't, of course, she reminded herself with a steadying clutch at her leather briefcase. She smiled brightly. "I'll get the keys to the Brewster property and be back in a few minutes."

Lil gave him the papers, and Tal took a seat by the broad expanse of glass wall. Shar felt inexplicably jittery when she walked into her private office. Because she felt she was doing something wrong? No, of course not. This was strictly business, on both sides. Nicole would no doubt be delighted when she learned that Shar and Tal had met in a very natural business way.

So why was she so nervous? The first thing she did after she located the Brewster keys was drop them. She then had to get down on hands and knees and scrunch under the desk to look for them. She hit her head and muttered "Damn" as she was backing out from under the desk.

And there was Tal peering down at her, amused by her undignified position. "May I help?"

Was he remembering another klutzy lady, who had spilled a drink all over herself?

"Everything is fine." She held up the keys, feeling oddly breathless, and brushed back the hair that had tumbled in a red-gold halo around her face. She had to get over this guilty, suspicious worry that he was suddenly going to recognize her. Even if he sensed some small similarities between her and a certain blond harem girl, what she had done Saturday night was so preposterous that he'd have to dismiss any similarities as pure coincidence. Thank heavens she'd worn that veil over the lower half of her face!

"The papers look fine," Tal said. He handed them to her. "I've signed them. But to be honest, I don't hold out much hope that you'll be able to do anything with my property. Things are pretty slow down there. I had the property listed with a broker there for three months and never got any action."

"I may run down and take a look at it."

"Really?" He looked surprised.

"Sometimes real estate offices handle out-of-town properties sight unseen, but I like to know what I'm selling. Or trading."

Shar dropped the papers on Lil's desk as they went out, getting a reproachful envious whisper in return. "Wish *I* got to spend the afternoon with a hunk like that."

Shar just smiled. Tal O'Neal was someone else's "hunk."

They went in Shar's car, a roomy sedan. Actually she'd have preferred something small and sporty like Tal's car, but she needed more space for hauling clients around.

They carried on impersonal small talk while driving to the Brewster Company property, touching lightly on the local construction scene and current economic conditions. She admitted that her knowledge of heavy equipment was limited and simply let him browse through the equipment descriptions himself. After a few minutes the muscles that felt as if they were wound around a lead bolt in her stomach finally began to relax.

She glanced at him surreptitiously as he read through the equipment descriptions. He'd taken off the raincoat, and his khaki work shirt was carelessly open at the throat, cuffs rolled back over lean forearms darkened with masculine hair. He had a superb physique that she suspected had been built by hard work, not by exercise simply for the sake of exercise. Corded throat, muscled shoulders, flat abdomen, a rangy grace. The air of a man who was unfailingly competent, and who expected the same from those around him. Even doing nothing more than sitting there reading, Tal possessed an exciting vitality, a leashed energy that kept him alert for action.

Was he as unaware of that potent male attractiveness as he seemed to be? No, she decided. In the appropriate setting he would know exactly how to use every inch of that toned male body. But he wouldn't go around flaunting a macho sexiness the way too many attractive men did, their enormous male egos demanding that they dazzle every woman within reach. His impact was natural, not manufactured.

He interrupted her mental wandering with a comment that the asking price of the Brewster property and equipment was somewhat above the value of his southern Oregon property.

"They may be willing to lower their price, but it's possible you'd have to come up with some additional cash." At the stoplight she slanted him a sideways glance. "Would that be a problem?"

"I'd rather not put out any additional cash, of course, but I could do it if the deal proved attractive enough."

A good answer, Shar reflected. It indicated that he was a careful businessman but one who was willing to take a worthwhile risk. It also meant, she realized as an afterthought, that her earlier suspicion had been unwarranted. Evidently he wasn't hurting for money, so he wouldn't be after Nicole for hers. Had the man no faults, she wondered with a small smile, no hidden shortcomings? Apparently not, but she was momentarily mindful of Nicole's wry comment that he sounded almost too good to be true.

He put the papers back in her briefcase as she turned the car into the driveway of the deserted-looking Brewster Company property. It was surrounded by a high metal-mesh security fence and a locked gate. Tal held out his hand for the keys, then unlocked the gate so that she could drive through. The property held a large warehouse with an office built onto the front. Some open empty sheds lined one side of the fence. A calico cat peered out of a shed, then dashed away at their approach. The equipment—a crane, bulldozer, backhoe and a couple of forklifts—stood near the fence like forlorn metal dinosaurs slowly turning to rust.

"It has a lot of possibilities," she offered, trying not to sound apologetic. She hadn't been out here in some time, and the property was beginning to look more abandoned than temporarily unused. Tal laughed and Shar had to join in. They both recognized the line for the cliché that it was. Yet the property did have possibilities, which she suspected Tal recognized, as well.

The rain was still coming down in silvery sheets, but a line of weak blue showed off to the west. "Let's take a look inside the building first," Tal suggested. "Maybe the rain will let up in a few minutes, and I'll go over the equipment then."

"There are keys to the equipment on that key ring, but I doubt that any of the engines have been started in some time."

Tal cast a dubious glance in the direction of the big crane. "From here, I'd suspect that Noah might have used that crane to help build the ark. And he probably bought it secondhand."

Shar laughed. "The equipment does look a little old," she admitted, deciding there was no point in making some heavy sales pitch. She figured that Tal was the kind of man who would make a deal for the property and equipment if he wanted them, and if he didn't want them, nothing she said would be apt to change his mind.

Locating the small umbrella she always carried in the car, she held it at an angle to the slanting rain and she picked her way around the shallow puddles in the uneven parking lot. She was wearing high-heeled burgundy boots, with beige pants and jacket.

Tal still had the keys. He unlocked the office door and pushed it open for her. The two rooms were bare and dusty. He inspected them briskly, Shar following. She shook a spray of raindrops from the umbrella. Beyond the office the door to the main warehouse area was ajar. Shar peered into the empty semidarkness beyond. Little windows lined the far wall, but they made only a small dent in the cavernous gloom. Above, a maze of rafters faded into total darkness. The place smelled damp and musty.

"Makes me feel like the doomed heroine in some horror movie, the one you just know the ax murderer is going to get as soon as she steps through the door," she murmured, laughing a little at her own apprehension. She flicked a row of light switches on the wall but nothing happened.

Tal laughed, too. "All we need is a little spooky mood music." Yet he stepped through the door without hesitation, obviously not intimidated by the gloomy ambience of the old warehouse. His footsteps made hollow echoes on the concrete floor. The enormous empty space should have diminished him, made him appear insignificant, but it didn't. He stood in the semidarkness like a commander, one who could take charge of all this and make it come alive with light and activity.

"Reminds me of the first warehouse my dad bought." His voice sounded hollow, too. He moved farther into the gloom until he was only a vague outline. "I guess they all have this feeling when they're unused and empty, kind of desolate and hopeless, like some underground cave you might get trapped in forever if you aren't careful."

Shar followed him, drawn by something in his voice plus a certain reluctance to be left totally alone here. The concrete felt cold and damp through the thin soles of her dress boots. The oblong of gray that marked the doorway to the office suddenly looked far away, and she had to blink her eyes to keep it from fading into the dark wall. She hoped there weren't bats or other unknown creatures lurking in the open rafters above. Rain pounded the roof, sounding like the muffled rumble of distant drums. It was the kind of place that made one want to seek the sound of a human voice, the warmth of a human hand.

"Is your father in the construction business, too?" she asked. She felt that if conversation faded away, she could be swallowed up by the emptiness of this place.

"We were in business together at one time, but he's dead now." The lonely shadows seemed to echo and magnify the quiet regret in Tal's voice.

"You must have been very close." His words brought to Shar a surge of her old, long-buried regret that her own father hadn't been the kind of man to encourage a close relationship.

"The business was his dream . . . but it killed him."

Shar felt a deepening curiosity and something more than that—a concern awakened by the unexpected sadness in his voice. But she didn't know whether to probe. Perhaps the setting, the semidarkness, the cold emptiness was affecting her, but she felt oddly melancholy, too. She had also had dreams, ones that didn't include being alone at twenty-eight, a career woman who presented such a glossy, self-assured, independent image to the world. She had the instinctive feeling that Tal would never have said what he just had about his father's dream if they had been face to face in normal light. There was a cut-off-from-the-world feeling here that drew out secrets, as if the emptiness had to be filled.

"His dream was to be in business with you?" Shar prompted softly.

"The construction business. Always the construction business. O'Neal and Son Construction, that was always his dream. I can remember him talking about it when I was just a kid and he was general handyman at a little country school. Not long after I got out of high school, he sold a piece of property that he'd bought when he and my mother first moved to southern Oregon. It was way out in the boondocks when he first bought it, but by the time he sold it expansion had caught up, and it had become rather valuable subdivision property. After he sold it his dream became a reality. O'Neal and Son Construction was in business."

"It's a dream many men have," Shar said. "To have a son who carries on a name and a business." She wondered silently if he had the same dream.

"We went great guns for a while. Too great. I kept telling Dad that we were spreading ourselves too thin and expanding too fast. But he didn't understand things like undercapitalization, and I hadn't the experience or sufficient control of the company to stop what he was doing. When the whole thing caved in on us, it took all the drive and steam out of him. It got so that we couldn't even pay our employees, which was when he went out to do some Cat work on a job himself." Tal stopped short, and even though Shar could barely see him in the gloom, the sound of his painful swallow reached her. "The 'dozer turned over on him and killed him."

Nothing she could say seemed even remotely adequate. She remained silent.

"I spent the next few years reorganizing the company and pulling it out of a financial mess. I didn't want to declare bankruptcy and put a black mark on my father's name."

Shar sensed raw determination in the quiet but fierce words. Tal wasn't the type to quit or admit defeat. He'd stand and fight no matter what it cost him. Now she understood what Nicole had said about his having been too tied up with business to have time for marriage. It wasn't just ruthless ambition or a quest for money that motivated him. Work was something he had to do, a loyalty and responsibility that came before all else.

"Your father would be proud of you," Shar said simply. "You have a solid thriving company that bears the O'Neal name, and he'd be proud."

Tal appeared beside her, his solid male frame materializing out of the shadows suddenly enough to startle her. He looked down at her, his head tilted. "No one has ever said that to me before. When it happened people said things about what a tragedy it was and how sorry they were. They were sincere and meant well, but somehow statements like that just made me feel frustrated. But thinking he'd be proud makes me feel the struggle and sacrifices were all worthwhile."

He leaned a little closer, as if for the first time seeing her as a flesh-and-blood woman rather than an impersonal real estate broker. A strange feeling flickered through Shar as he looked at her so intently, a reaction she rejected even before it could be identified.

Then he laughed a little self-consciously. "I don't know what got me started on all that. I haven't even mentioned my father to anyone in a long time. Do you run a little self-help psychology business on the side?"

"It isn't me; it's the place. It's the kind of place that encourages . . . confidences." Lightly, to get away from the seriousness and disturbing intimacy of the moment, she added, "If you buy it, perhaps you could rent it out to one of those bare-your-soul encounter groups."

"I don't hear *you* sharing any confidences."

Shar had a sudden, almost irresistible urge to spill out a lifetime of her own dreams gone awry, of hurts and disillusionments, of picking herself up and starting over again, of wishing that someone solid and dependable would come into her life to share her hard-won accomplishments and add the love that made life dance instead of plod. She didn't, of course. What she said was "I think the rain may have let up. Do you want to go look at the equipment now?"

He stood there a moment longer, as if he were half-inclined to press for some revealing intimacy from her; then he simply nodded and started toward the office door. He asked some casual questions about property taxes and the age and past use of the building, then commented on the solid construction.

Once in the office, Tal headed directly for the outside entrance, but Shar paused. Their tracks made a tangled pattern on the dusty floor, subtly hinting at more intimacy than had existed.

At one point her boot prints faced the heavier outline of his tracks beneath a window, so close together that it looked as if they had shared a passionate embrace. Which they hadn't, of course; it was merely an illusion. He had stood there alone at one moment; she had paused there a few moments later.

This raised an odd thought, a musing on the vagaries of fate and time. If their lives had crossed at a different point in time...if she hadn't gone away to Los Angeles...if she instead of Nicole had met him first—

Abruptly she tossed away those irrelevant and dangerous thoughts.

"You go on ahead," she called to him. "I'll lock up and meet you at the car."

Tal tossed the keys to her and strode off across the puddled parking lot. He had a graceful, loose, ground-
covering walk, Shar thought. A purposeful man, a man
who rumor said could be ruthless under certain conditions, a man who knew where he was going and what he
wanted and didn't waste time about it. No wonder Nicole
had that slightly dazed, swept-off-her-feet look.

Shar started toward the main exit, then took a moment
to return to the warehouse door. It should be closed to
keep the damp musty odor from permeating the office
area. She had her hand on the knob when a small noise
caught her attention.

The squeaking of a mouse or rat? No. It was something
more plaintive than that, more like a forlorn mewing. Had
the calico cat come inside? This big barn of a place was
hardly catproof.

"Kitty, kitty, kitty?" she called tentatively into the
gloom.

The sound stopped, then came again the same as before, plaintively repetitious. It definitely sounded like a
cat, but hardly the big self-reliant creature she'd seen outside. She walked a few feet into the dim cavern and turned
in a slow circle as she tried to locate the source of the
sound.

It was above her, she finally decided. A cat trapped on
a high rafter, unable to find a way down? She repeated the
tentative call, remembering how her old tom used to answer her call with a cranky yowl, then would finally appear and consent grudgingly to her gentle stroking of his
battle-scarred hide.

This mewing had none of old Slugger's cranky inde-
pendence, however. It sounded a little hoarse, as if it had
been going on for a long time. Hoarse and hopeless.

Shar walked the length of the wall, dragging her fingers along the rough wooden partition that separated the office area from the cavernous warehouse. Then her hand encountered a protrusion. She stepped back, trying to make out what it was. It was a ladder, the rough rungs made out of two-by-fours nailed to timbers fastened directly to the wall. Where did it go? Perhaps the area above the office had been used for storage.

She slung the straps of her handbag over her shoulder and started climbing upward. The mewing grew louder, not, she thought, because the animal's cries were growing stronger, but because she was getting closer. A sliver from the rough wood rammed painfully into her forefinger, and she paused to rest and nurse the injured spot by lightly sucking on it.

"Kitty, kitty? Are you up here? What are you doing up here?"

The mewing stopped, as if the creature was suddenly afraid of being found. Shar cautiously edged upward into the darkness, uncertain if her head might clunk into a rafter at any moment or, worse, if she might find herself tangled in a mass of spiderwebs, the owners in residence.

Finally her upraised hand found no more rungs on the ladder, and she cautiously climbed over the edge. Then she remembered the little penlight that she always kept in her handbag. Fishing it out, she played the narrow beam over the dusty boards, shuddering a little at the silvery jungle of cobwebs laced between floor and angled rafters. And then the flashlight caught the gleam of eyes from what was surely the darkest and most remote corner. A weak but defiant hiss followed.

"Here, kitty, kitty," she coaxed gently. "Come on out. This is no place for a kitty." She could now make out the shadowy form of a half-grown kitten. "Why are you so afraid? I won't hurt you."

She squatted, edging as far as she could under the sloping rafters and using a broken board to fend off cobwebs. She was still several feet from the kitten. At that point it occurred to her that it had probably been born and raised right here without benefit of human help, and she was probably terrifying the poor little thing with her presence. She started to back away, but then an odd clattering sound came from the corner. She targeted the narrow flashlight beam more closely and gasped with horror. One of the kitten's front paws was caught in the cruel grip of a big rattrap, evidently left over from when the warehouse had been in use.

Shar gave only a moment's thought to her expensive beige outfit before getting down on her knees and finally wriggling along on her stomach to reach the animal. She got her hands on the bit of fur and ribs, only to discover that the rattrap was anchored to the floor with a length of heavy cord. She couldn't break the cord, and she couldn't budge the metal part of the trap to free the kitten.

"Hey, where'd you go?" The voice floated up to her from below. "I've been looking all over for you."

"I'm up here, above the office," Shar called back, feeling the frightened kitten flinch at the sound of her voice. "There's a kitten caught in a rattrap up here. Do you have a pocket knife?"

"Sure. How'd you get up there?"

Shar directed him to the ladder, and a few minutes later she felt the vibration of his footsteps through the boards she was lying against. "If you'll toss me the knife I'll try to cut the cord that's holding the trap," she said over her shoulder. "You can't stand up back here."

To her surprise, a moment later he was on the floor beside her, his body brushing hers as he shouldered his way to within reaching distance of the cord. He smelled damp and warm and male, infinitely reassuring after Shar's momentary feeling of utter helplessness. His braced thigh, hard and warm, touched hers as he quickly slashed through the cord with his sharp knife. Shar had been holding her head up, and now she let it drop limply on her closed fist. The kitten was motionless, evidently too terrified at the moment to struggle.

"How the hell did you ever find a kitten trapped way up here?" He lifted his arm, and in the cramped space it came down around her shoulders, his fingers tangling in the silky length of her hair.

"I heard it mewing and started looking for it."

She edged backward until she could sit up under the sloping roof. He followed, and they sat crosslegged with knees touching, the kitten, one paw still cruelly clamped in the grip of the rattrap, between them.

"You hold the kitten while I slip the blade of my knife under the trap and free its paw. It looks as if it may try to run, and it's going to need medical attention."

Shar nodded, her disheveled hair tumbling across her face. She clasped both hands around the pitifully thin kitten, her heart aching at the thought of how long it may have been trapped there. Tal targeted the pencil of light on the trap and then, with delicate skill, worked the blade of the knife between the metal and wooden parts of the trap, finally forcing them apart and freeing the kitten's paw.

Shar clutched the poor little creature to her chest, cradling it with the warmth of her body and feeling the terrified patter of its heart. She suspected this was the first time the wild little thing had ever been held.

Tal closed the knife and shoved it back into his pants pocket. "Somehow I didn't figure you for the kind of woman who'd get herself and her expensive clothes dirty rescuing a trapped kitten."

"Dirty clothes don't bother me, but spiders do," she admitted.

"In fact, you're not at all what I expected when I first talked to you on the phone," he added.

"What did you expect?"

"Someone very hard and businesslike. Certainly someone who would be more concerned about her makeup than about a stray cat."

"I couldn't just leave it here, alone and suffering," Shar protested. "Neither could you," she added intuitively.

"True." His smile flashed in the dim glow of the tiny light. "But don't tell the guys who work for me. They think I'm tough enough to chew nails."

That really came as no surprise to Shar. It only reaffirmed the impression she had of him based on what Nicole had said and her own observations. A man who was strong but tender, a man who had complex layers of unexplored character. Their knees were still touching, and oddly Shar was more affected by the small accidental contact than she would have been by some overeager date's aggressive caresses. She was conscious of the hard solidity of bone, an appealing knobbiness, of a fleeting impression of the warm comfort of a leg thrown over her in the night. There was an intimate familiarity about the meeting of such ordinary nonerotic parts of the body, as if the small experience they had just shared had made unnecessary the usual feints and thrusts of a man and woman getting to know each other, had instantly put the two of them on some more intimate basis.

No, it had simply made them friends, Shar told herself resolutely. Friends.

Hastily she scooted away to a point where the rafters were high enough so that she could stand up. But when she did, a strand of hair caught on the rough wood. She struggled, trying to free it with one hand, and then Tal came to her rescue.

"Here, let me do that." With deft, capable fingers he painlessly separated the silky hair from the rafter. Shar had the peculiar feeling that the individual strands of her hair had suddenly developed nerves, nerves that sent little tingles shooting into her scalp.

"What are you planning to do with the kitten?" he asked as he smoothed the tangled strands back into place.

"Get it to a vet as soon as possible. Then take it home when it's well." She stroked the bony ridge of the kitten's spine. It had either given up or was too weak to struggle anymore and simply burrowed into the warmth of her body.

"Can you do that? So many places don't allow pets."

"I have a...very understanding landlord." Shar smiled to herself, not explaining that she was that very understanding landlord.

"We'd better get going, then."

He started down the vertical ladder first, hooking one arm over a rung and using his other hand to guide her foot to a rung. Slowly they worked their way downward, their progress awkward because Shar had only one hand free. There was an enforced intimacy to their movements. Bodies lightly colliding on the narrow ladder, hand and leg touching as he guided her feet from one rung to the next. The accidental brush of his palm over her buttocks when his hand moved up to brace her waist. By now her blouse had come out of the band of her pants, and once his hand slipped underneath to bare skin. She had the uncomfortable feeling that there were invisible forces conspiring to make them physically aware of each other in every way possible.

There was no conversation except for his occasional instruction for her to move her foot a little lower or higher, a question if she was okay. Shar tried to ignore the accidental contacts. She didn't believe he was taking advantage of the opportunity, as some men in such a situation might have done. The touches neither lingered nor explored. Yet she had the instinctive feeling that he was as electrically aware of them as she was. Her breasts were taut, prickly and aroused by the nearness of his hands and body.

When he had both feet solidly on the concrete, he put his hands on her waist to help her take the last step downward. She stumbled a little and fell back against him. His arms went around her, strong, capable, reassuring. She felt his breath on her temple, his cheek against her hair. Her free hand caught the back of his fingers, and she clung for a moment, desperately wishing—

Instantly she rejected the yearning that welled up like some geyser from deep inside her. She stepped free, as if she had merely been using her grip on his hand to brace herself.

"Well, that was a little tricky, wasn't it? Thanks for all your help." She took deep deliberate gulps of the musty air to rid herself of that breathless feeling.

The kitten was so motionless now that only the frantic hammering of its heart assured Shar that it was still alive. She blinked when they entered the unexpected brightness of the office. A weak sun glimmered outside. Shar looked at Tal and unexpectedly burst out laughing.

"What's so funny?"

"You."

Silvery cobwebs netted his hair and tangled in his eyebrows, giving his dark good looks a demonic cast—but the results were more comic than frightening. Dust smudged his temple and an angular cheekbone, and there was a rip in his raincoat. The sudden sparkle in his eyes was more boyish than satanic.

"And I suppose you think you are still the elegant picture-perfect image of Real Estate Person of the Year?" he inquired.

Shar looked down at the dusty streaks on her beige pants and jacket. The knees and elbows were the worst. She looked as if she had been crawling around in a dirty attic, which was exactly what she had been doing, of course. She smiled and blew at a cobweb dangling across her face. "Maybe I've carried this year's casual look in fashion a little too far?" she asked with mock concern.

He reached over and wiped a finger across a dark smudge on her cheek. She thought he was going to say something teasing, but he didn't. His hand slid up to brush the hair and cobwebs out of her eyes, and his voice was gravely tender when he said, "Whatever it is, I like it."

Her green eyes stared into the depths of his, where green-brown mingled with flecks of gold. Where she saw a warmth and interest that had nothing to do with her ability as a real estate trader. Where a potential for passion that she had always known was there lurked with gleaming intensity....

4

FOR A MOMENT Shar felt dizzy, as if the world had unexpectedly tilted beneath her feet. Then her mind swiftly interjected the barrier of Nicole, breaking the electricity arcing between them.

Quickly she said, "I know you must be in a hurry to get back to work."

"Why don't we take the kitten to the veterinarian's office first?" Tal suggested.

"It's out of the way, and I may have to wait to get in to see the vet."

"I don't mind." He smiled in friendly conspiracy. "I'm the boss. No one is going to fire me if I don't get back on time. I'll drive, and you can hold the kitten."

He took easy command of the situation, locking doors and gate, sliding behind the wheel and efficiently picking the shortest route to the address Shar had given him for the veterinarian. The kitten made a small warm spot against her breast, sheltered under the protection of her jacket. The frantic pattering of its heart had slowed, but the feline wasn't yet secure enough to purr.

They had to wait more than an hour before getting in to see the vet. After a half hour Shar suggested that Tal drive her car back to the office, where he could get his pickup, and she'd take a taxi later. But he brushed the offer aside. He read a magazine with apparent patience despite the lengthy delay.

Shar was sharply conscious of his presence in the chair next to her. Why was he staying? Out of concern for the kitten? Because he wanted to discuss a trade on the Brewster property? Occasionally his thigh brushed hers as he shifted weight in the hard plastic chair, heightening her awareness of him and sending small shock waves through her leg. Once he leaned over to show her an amusing cartoon in a pet magazine, warming her with his chuckle; another time he asked if she'd like coffee from the McDonald's across the street.

She was about to take him up on that offer when the receptionist finally called her into the examining room. Tal followed.

"Another stray in distress?" Dr. Haley inquired with a smile. Shar had been there before with unfortunate creatures. The attractive veterinarian made a noncritical inspection of Shar's disheveled condition. "Looks as if you climbed a tree or something to get this one."

"Almost," Shar agreed. She reached under her jacket for the kitten, but by now the small animal had decided this was a safe haven and had no intention of leaving it. The claws in its three good paws clung with surprising tenacity to Shar's blouse, even invading to prick her skin. "Ouch!"

"Let me help." Tal reached under the kitten to disentangle the tiny but sharp claws, and his knuckles brushed Shar's breast. To hide an inappropriate catch of breath and an even less appropriate firming of soft flesh beneath the accidental touch of his hand, Shar said quickly, "Dr. Haley, this is Tal O'Neal, a client from the office. He unfortunately got involved in the rescue operation. We found the kitten caught in a rattrap in an old storage area."

"I don't consider my involvement so unfortunate," Tal disagreed mildly after acknowledging the introduction with a nod. He got the two small hind feet trapped in one hand, then gently worked the third paw free. Finally he set the small creature on the gleaming metal examining table. Shar self-consciously buttoned her dust-streaked jacket over her smudged, claw-pricked blouse, but it wasn't really the condition of the blouse that made her feel self-conscious.

The kitten made no move to escape. It huddled, small and terrified, on the expanse of shiny metal, but it still hissed defiantly. This was the first good look Shar had got of her new pet. It was a pretty kitten in spite of its pitifully thin condition, a calico colorfully marked with orange, white and black. And Shar admired that feisty spark of defiance.

Dr. Haley efficiently but gently examined the kitten. She said the mangled paw couldn't be saved and would have to be amputated. Shar made arrangements to have the surgery performed the following morning and said she'd stop by later in the day to check on her new pet. She gave the kitten a final encouraging caress before entrusting it to the veterinarian.

Shar washed her hands before leaving the vet's office, but that didn't get rid of the dusty, cobwebby feeling or the dirty streaks on her clothing. Also, the finger with the sliver in it ached.

"Would you like that cup of coffee now?" Tal asked. "Or perhaps you'd just like to go home and change clothes before going back to the office?"

Shar definitely wanted to get out of the dirty clothes, and she needed a cup of coffee. It was on the tip of her tongue to suggest that they go by her place and fix coffee there while she changed clothes, but she held the words back. For a moment she had almost forgotten that this was the man Nicole was in love with. Her relationship with him had already slipped beyond strictly impersonal bounds, and it mustn't go farther. Also, she must not let him realize that she and a certain blond sexpot shared the same address.

Suddenly Shar urgently needed to get away from Tal, to turn and run before . . . before what? She glanced up at him as he opened the car door, her eyes uncharacteristically uncertain. What was it that she was afraid might happen? He'd already proven himself to be loyal and faithful to Nicole. It was something else, some hovering emotion within that emitted warning vibrations.

Yet there was also the memory of that warm light of interest in his eyes out at the Brewster warehouse and of her and Tal's potent awareness of each other's bodies.

"Thanks, but I keep a change of clothes at the office, and I really should get back." Brightly she added, "There's coffee at the office, if you'd like a cup there."

They were in the car before she realized that he had taken the driver's seat again. He was a man who automatically took charge. She was momentarily annoyed—she wasn't helpless—then succumbed to the greater luxury of letting someone else cope with late-afternoon city traffic. She leaned her head against the padded headrest.

"You make a habit of rescuing stray animals?" Tal inquired as they started across town to Shar's office. "You and the vet seem to know each other."

"Not habit. It's more a matter of inopportune timing." She started to explain about old Slugger . . . and the terrier she'd seen hit by a car . . . and the owl she'd found injured in the woods. Then she stopped. None of this was relevant to their business relationship. Quickly she changed the subject. "What did you think of the Brewster property?"

"I'll consider it, although I'm not wildly enthusiastic. I'd be more interested if the equipment were in better condition. Have you anything else?"

"At the moment I can't think of anyone who has specifically indicated an interest in trading for southern Oregon property, but I'll call several of my clients and ask if they're open to the idea. We don't, of course, have to consider just direct trades."

"Oh?" He expertly maneuvered around a stalled car and gave her an interested glance.

"I've handled trades involving as many as six separate properties." Shar felt on firmer ground here, out of the quicksand of personal questions and involvement. She straightened in the seat and went on to explain a bit about the complicated process of trading, using as an example a recent transaction she had arranged in which the owner of a Portland motel wanted an eastern Oregon ranch. But the ranch owner had wanted nothing to do with the headaches of running a motel. Another client had been trying to sell his equity in a large office building farther north, in Vancouver. "I linked them all, so the motel owner got the ranch, the ranch owner got the office building—and turned it over to a professional management agency that I recommended, so he could spend his time fishing—and the office building owners got the motel."

"And the real estate salesperson gets a commission from each property owner, I take it?"

"There may be several brokers involved in a complicated trade, so it isn't as if one salesperson gets all the commissions. These trades may also take a considerable amount of time to set up. They don't happen overnight."

"But it is a rather lucrative field."

"We earn the money!"

Tal laughed. "You needn't be so defensive. I'm not criticizing. I admire someone with the initiative and creativity to handle something like that. It's a little like fitting the pieces of a puzzle together, except that you have to supply the pieces yourself. And there is certainly nothing wrong with being in a lucrative line of work. How did you happen to get into the real estate field?"

"I dropped out of college in the middle of my junior year—"

"Where did you go to college?" he interrupted.

"The University of Washington, up in Seattle. When I dropped out I went to work as a receptionist in a real estate office here in Portland. I actually intended to stay with the job only temporarily, until I . . ." Shar hesitated, then backtracked to change her phrasing. She had no intention of explaining to him that she had taken the job only as a stopgap measure while trying to cope with the devastating effects of what Matt had done to her. "But I became very interested in real estate and decided to study for a license so I could sell. Later I joined the firm I'm with now, and a couple of years ago I passed the broker's exam."

"So with a broker's license you could be in business on your own rather than working for someone else."

Shar hesitated, relieved that he hadn't asked why she had come to Portland after dropping out of college in Seattle, but uneasily feeling that he was somehow doing more than checking out her professional credentials. "Actually, I'm a junior partner in the firm now."

There was nothing in his next comment to confirm her suspicion. "That's very impressive. And how did you happen to start specializing in trades?"

"More or less by accident."

"Sometimes the best things happen by accident." She stiffened as she thought for a moment that he was going to apply that remark to something personal between them, but he merely added, "It was more or less by accident that I moved my business here to Portland. I'd planned to enter the modular construction field in the Medford area. Then a plant that was already set up for building modular units became available here. So I revised my plans."

"I think the modular construction field has a lot of potential. It was my impression that Madrona failed more because of management problems than lack of opportunity."

"Is that a warning or a vote of confidence?" he inquired with a sideways glance and a smile as he turned into the parking lot at Shar's office. He nosed the car into a parking slot next to his pickup and turned off the engine.

"Just an expression of hope for good luck with your new venture. I'll be in touch after I check into some further trade possibilities for your southern Oregon property," Shar said.

Tal glanced at his watch. "It's almost five o'clock. How late do you work?"

"I don't keep set hours. I often work evenings to accommodate the hours my clients have available."

"Are you working this evening?" he persisted. "After you change into the clothes you said you keep here?"

Shar retrieved her briefcase from the floorboard. Again she had the uneasy feeling that he was trying to expand their relationship beyond the business area. She wondered if she had assured Nicole too soon that he was totally dependable, steadfastly faithful and reliable. Reluctantly she said, "I'd have to check my calendar."

He confirmed her uneasy suspicions.

"I was just thinking that perhaps I could take you to dinner, either now, if you don't mind eating early, or later, if you'd prefer."

Shar didn't look at him, didn't want to see a gleam of seductive interest in his green-brown eyes, didn't want to see a smile that promised exciting after-dinner diversions. A hard knot formed in her stomach, a painful lump of disappointment and dismay. Her suspicions had been neither unwarranted nor unfair. He wasn't some saint, after all; he was as human and susceptible as any other man. He didn't happen to like aggressive blondes, but he wasn't averse to fun and games with one slightly disheveled redhead. She should have realized that all along. He was too good-looking, too ruggedly attractive, too smoothly experienced. Too male.

Later she'd have to think about how to break this to Nicole, but for now she just wanted to escape.

"No, thanks." She slid out of the car, not bothering to soften the turndown with explanations. A technique he would probably recognize, she thought bitterly as she slammed the car door behind her.

"You're sure?" he called from the far side of the car, evidently missing the curtness of her response. "Perhaps I could have your clothes cleaned, then."

Shar turned to look at him, confused. What did cleaning her clothes have to do with asking her to dinner?

"I'm sorry about your getting them dirty. It's a very attractive outfit, and I feel responsible for the damage. I just thought I could make it up to you by taking you to dinner or something." He smiled disarmingly. "You haven't had a chance to see the seat of those pants yet. They're worse than the front."

"It wasn't your fault! I was the one who crawled up there looking for the kitten."

"I know, but if you hadn't been showing me the property it wouldn't have happened. I really would like to make it up to you some way."

You just have, Shar thought. *You've just proved to me that nice guys really do exist, that not every guy is out to score.*

He stepped around the hood of the car. "Look, do you really want to keep the kitten? Or would you rather find someone else to take it? I know a little girl who would love to have it. Maybe I could do that much to help out."

He must mean Nicole's daughter, Shar realized. She was mentally accusing him of all sorts of devious underhanded schemes, and he really was just trying to do something helpful because he felt responsible for her smudged clothing. Shar was suddenly ashamed of herself. Perhaps it was her own soiled thoughts that needed dry cleaning. She had read something into the dinner invitation that hadn't been there at all. Tal O'Neal might have the dashing good looks of a bedroom adventurer, but he was *nice*. It was time she accepted that without suspecting some ulterior motive behind his every friendly considerate move.

However, there was one thing she knew that Tal obviously didn't. Nicole was allergic to both cat and dog hair, so that Cindy had never been able to have a pet. Shar was on the verge of telling him that and confessing everything about the masquerade. He had a sense of humor; he'd probably think the entire escapade uproariously funny.

Yet he hadn't acquired that reputation for a certain degree of ruthlessness by being a nice guy all the time, and she didn't really know how he'd react to such an unlikely revelation. Prudently she decided to let the matter drop. She didn't want to say something that could damage Nicole's relationship with him. Perhaps Nicole herself would someday tell him about the outrageous seduction test.

Shar smiled. "Yes, I really do want to keep the kitten myself. No, I don't want you to have my clothes cleaned.

Getting them dirty wasn't your fault. It's just something that occasionally goes with the job. I probably should have worn something different." Shar hesitated before responding to his other suggestion. Would there really be anything so wrong with simply sharing a dinner with him? She occasionally dined with other clients.

But Tal wasn't just another client.

"And, no, I—I can't have dinner with you," she added with a certain regret.

"Any particular reason?"

"A . . . personal matter."

He considered the answer briefly before tilting his head. "Jealous boyfriend?"

Shar's lips twitched as she held back a smile. Tal was so nice that if she said there was a jealous boyfriend he would probably invite him along, too. "No." She couldn't explain the "personal matter," but she didn't feel inclined to manufacture some phony excuse, either. So she simply said, "Thanks, anyway, for the invitation."

Her regret deepened as she watched the big pickup pull out of the parking lot. She would have liked to have had dinner with Tal. She would have liked to have talked about kittens in warehouses and tenth wedding anniversaries and devoting too much of life to work. She would have liked to have met his eyes over a candlelit table and heard his warm husky laugh, felt the rough competent touch of his hands and the embrace of strong arms. She would have liked—

Shar's thoughts skidded to a halt before she could dip any farther into the hazy depths of her yearnings. Before those unexpected guilty yearnings became too explicit.

But it wasn't really Tal himself that she was fantasizing about, she assured herself. Just a man somewhat *like* Tal, someone warm and tender, dependable and faithful. Nicole was one very lucky woman to have found herself such a rare man. Wasn't it great, in fact, that two of the nicest people she knew had found each other?

Shar felt a wetness on her lashes. "Raining again," she grumbled as she blinked vigorously...even though the sky overhead was now a soft clear blue.

SHE CALLED NICOLE from her desk phone a few minutes later, punching the numbers with the blunt end of a ballpoint pen because her finger with the sliver embedded in it still hurt. She told Nicole in detail all about Tal's unexpected phone call, about showing him the warehouse and finding the kitten.

"Shar, that's fabulous! And he never suspected a thing about having met you before, did he? I told you he wouldn't."

"I think our secret is safe."

"Then let's all get together this weekend. How about dinner at my house? Then we'll run something interesting on the VCR."

"Nikkie, haven't you heard that great old saying, 'three's a crowd'?"

"You can bring a date—"

"Four is an even larger crowd. I'm sure the last thing in the world Tal would like to see is his real estate agent plopped on your living room sofa, with or without a date."

"Oh, darn, I just remembered," Nicole broke in. "We can't get together this weekend, anyway. Tal and I are invited to a big dinner party at the Wheelers' home Saturday night. It's nice to have a social life again. I've hidden at home much too long."

Shar nibbled the end of her pen while Nicole bubbled on with details about the dinner party and the man who was to be guest of honor, an artist from back East who was gaining fame for his strange paintings of pale elongated female forms. Shar listened in silence before saying doubtfully, "Nikkie, are you really sure Tal likes this sort of thing?"

"Dave always said he made his most useful business contacts at dinners, and there will be lots of important people at this one."

"I know, but Tal is in an entirely different line of work than Dave was, and Tal . . . isn't Dave. Maybe he'd rather just be with you than with a whole crowd of people he doesn't know."

"Are you trying to tell me he's antisocial or something?"

"Oh, no, Nikkie. Of course not. He's a terrific guy." *And what do I know about his likes or dislikes,* Shar added to herself. Nicole had been seeing Tal for some weeks now and undoubtedly knew him better than Shar did after only an evening and afternoon together.

"He is terrific, isn't he? I'd almost forgotten that wonderful dancing-on-air feeling a man can give you." Nicole's voice sounded youthfully dreamy, unmarred by unhappy experiences of the past.

"You sound like a woman in love." Nicole needed someone like Tal, Shar thought. Someone strong and protective to shield her from the harsh bumps of life.

"I guess I am," Nicole agreed. "Thanks to you."

"Thanks to me?"

"I think I've been falling in love with Tal ever since I met him, but I was afraid to really let myself go, and love him. . . . You know what I mean? But now I think I can." Nicole laughed a little breathlessly. "May second-time brides wear white?"

Shar swallowed past a peculiar thickness in her throat at the image of Tal standing tall and proud beside Nicole in a dazzling wedding dress. Loyally she said, "You can do anything you want to do, Nikkie."

"I want you and Tal to like each other," Nicole said firmly. "So we'll all get together sometime very soon. Okay?"

"We'll see," Shar murmured.

As she hung up the phone, however, Shar was certain she wasn't going to get involved in any chummy social activities with Tal and Nicole. She was delighted that Nicole was her old bright, bubbly self again; she was happy that Nicole had found a terrific man to love; she wished them both the best. But there was something about the prospect of socializing with the two of them once they'd become an intimate couple that rubbed her the wrong way, like sandpaper on raw skin.

SHAR HAND WASHED THE BLOUSE that evening and left the beige jacket and pants at the cleaners on the way to work the following day. She had a full morning of appointments but nevertheless ran over to Dr. Haley's office at lunchtime. The kitten was snuggled into a bed of shredded paper in a wire cage, peacefully sleeping off the effects of the anesthetic. The veterinarian thought it would pull through satisfactorily, although it hadn't been in the best condition for surgery.

Shar opened the cage door and gently stroked the kitten's thin body. She already felt a protective affection for the unfortunate little creature and silently promised better things to come. The bandaged leg looked almost too heavy a burden for the frail body to carry. Dr. Haley wanted to keep the kitten for a few days, and Shar said she'd check on it again the next day.

Back at the office Shar called several people to suggest a trade for Tal's southern Oregon property. She got only negative responses. She was interrupted by the arrival of a couple who had decided to go ahead with a pending four-way trade of houses and condos if the deal could be completed within a very short time. Shar then discovered that another of the owners involved, a couple, was away on vacation. She had to use her best detective skills to track them down via a series of long-distance telephone calls, all the time aware that, as the legal documents she frequently dealt with usually said, time was "of the essence."

When she finally located the couple that evening at a Tahoe resort, the transaction fell neatly into place, giving her the surge of exhilaration that always came with the successful arrangement of a deal. The exhilaration was tempered, though, by the knowledge that until all the papers were signed, the deal could always fall through; it had happened before. But she had a good feeling about this arrangement; it felt right.

She was less positive about working out something successful for Tal, although, as she had warned him, complicated trades did take time. She had a network of out-of-town contacts from past transactions and so put out several letters as feelers. Then she looked at the phone number on the listing Tal had given her. Should she call him? She really had nothing to tell him yet, but she usually kept in touch with clients to let them know she was working on a project, even if there were no promising prospects in sight at that moment.

She didn't call Tal. Maybe, she thought uneasily, because the prospect of hearing his husky voice on the phone held too much appeal? That was unthinkable, of course. And ridiculous. A woman didn't refrain from calling a man because she *wanted* to hear his voice.

Unless, perhaps, that man belonged to someone else....

The problem, she told herself firmly, was that she'd been seeing too few eligible men lately. She hadn't even had a date since coming back from California.

That situation righted itself when a man she had met in Ventura unexpectedly called to say he'd be in town on Friday evening. Would she have dinner with him? Under different conditions Shar would probably have politely rejected the invitation. Doug Morrison was an aggressive type of guy who probably thought their two casual dates in Ventura entitled him to a night in her apartment when he was passing through Portland. Still she could handle that; she was expert at smoothly detouring such situations.

And maybe it was time she didn't detour all of them, she reminded herself. Doug was attractive and fun. Perhaps, under his rather egotistical exterior, he was as nice as Tal. She optimistically accepted the invitation and gave Doug her home address.

ON FRIDAY AFTERNOON Shar picked up her jacket and pants from the cleaners. She drove around to the veterinarian's office to visit Tripod, who was already turning into a sassy, affectionate charmer. Shar had hoped to take the kitten home that day, but Dr. Haley wanted to keep her until Monday or Tuesday. Dr. Haley also said she was considering investing in some rental property, and when Shar went back to the office she made a list of several good buys that were available.

She was just preparing to call Dr. Haley back when Lil buzzed, informing her that Tal O'Neal was there to see her. "He says he doesn't have an appointment, but if you have a minute?"

Shar hesitated, her indecision quickly followed by annoyance with herself. Tal was a client; no doubt he was merely checking to see why she hadn't been in touch. But he could have called instead of dropping in and catching her unprepared. Then she had to stop and wonder . . . unprepared for what?

Briskly she answered, "Of course, send him right in."

Tal appeared in the doorway a moment later. "Hi. Hope I'm not interrupting something. I was over this way talking to a new lumber supplier and thought I'd drop in, since I hadn't heard from you."

Shar straightened and set aside the papers with the information for Dr. Haley, using the moment to neutralize the jolt she'd felt when he stepped into her office. No man should be so outrageously handsome, smile so irresistibly, light up her office with just his presence. A fresh rain-swept scent came with him, more appealing to Shar than the most expensive male cologne.

He was wearing the same raincoat he'd worn when they had gone out to the Brewster property together; Shar recognized the tiny rip the plastic had acquired that day. It gave her a small odd feeling of shared pasts, of knowing an intimate little detail about him that no one else knew. She quickly brushed away the feeling. He was merely a client, albeit more attractive than most.

"I haven't called because I really haven't had anything to tell you. You've decided against the Brewster property, I take it?"

"I've bought a crane, so now I don't need the equipment that went with the deal, and the property itself doesn't particularly appeal to me."

"Why don't you look through our current listings then and see if anything interests you? If it does, I can approach the owners about a possible trade."

Shar handed him a photocopied sheet with a summation of the more important details of the nonresidential

properties the firm currently had listed. This wasn't the
way she handled most clients. She had found that select-
ing one or two suitable properties and zeroing in on them
was more effective than overwhelming a client with too
many choices. But Tal wasn't her everyday client. She was
even aware of the moment when his fingers touched the
paper she handed to him, as if a current had flowed across
the page between them.

A new thought occurred to her. "But perhaps it isn't just
commerical or industrial property that interests you," she
suggested as he settled into a chair across from her. Would
he move into Nicole's house after they were married, or
would he want something new, something she hadn't
shared with another husband? "A house, perhaps?"

"No, I don't think so. My apartment is about all the
housekeeping I can manage alone." He spoke rather absentmindedly, a small crease between his heavy eyebrows
as he considered the listings.

So it was to be Nicole's house, then, which was certainly more than adequate even if they decided to increase the size of their family. And Tal surely had too much
self-confidence to be intimidated by the ghost of some
previous husband.

Suddenly he looked up, catching her studying him. The
moment of unexpected eye contact flustered Shar, as if
she'd been caught doing something she shouldn't have. She
fervently wished there was something she could find to
dislike about the man. Not something so terrible as to
make him unsuitable for Nicole, but something unlikable
enough to rid her of this small impossible attraction to
him. He couldn't be perfect, surely, and resentfully she almost wished he'd reveal a few cracks in his seemingly
flawless armor.

"I also wanted to ask, how's the injured kitten?"

"She's doing fine. I should be able to take her home Monday. I named her Tripod."

"Very appropriate. I'm glad she's all right." He returned to a perusal of the listings.

Shar sighed. The man had even remembered to inquire about a stray cat. But he must have *some* secret vices. Perhaps he was mean to his mother. Cheated his employees. Snored like a chain saw. She sighed again, suppressing wry amusement. She doubted the first two, and she'd never know about the third.

Tal took a pen out of his plaid work shirt and checked half a dozen items on the list. "Those I've marked might be possibilities," he said as he handed the sheets back to her. "One thing I don't believe I mentioned is that I might be interested in a vacation cabin over on the coast, if you happen to run across something like that."

He must have Nicole in mind. Nicole's grandparents had had a summer cabin on the Washington State coast, if something with four bedrooms and a sunken living room could really be called a cabin. Shar had spent one college spring vacation there with Nicole and several other girls. Shar and Nicole both loved the coast. However Nicole preferred to view a stormy sea from behind a picture window, and Shar liked to prowl the beach in the rain, dodging the assault of a tempestuous sea, searching for the small treasures washed in by the surf and tasting the salty spray on her lips.

"I'll keep it in mind," Shar said, reminding herself to run over to the coast again one of these days. "Would you like to look at any of these other properties?"

"Perhaps in a few days. I'll call you." He started toward the door, then glanced back. "I still owe you that dinner. I don't suppose you'd care to have it tonight?"

"You don't owe my any dinner," Shar protested. She stood up, fingertips spread lightly on the desk. "I got my clothes back from the cleaner's today, and the dirt streaks came out beautifully. Even my finger is nearly healed."

"I didn't know you'd hurt your finger. What happened?"

"I just got a sliver in it when I was climbing the ladder." Shar chastised herself for even mentioning the finger; it was totally irrelevant to the business relationship she was striving to establish.

"Let me see."

Suddenly he was standing beside her on her side of the desk, and his nearness unnerved her. She tried to take a step backward, but her swivel chair blocked retreat. Feeling utterly foolish, she put the hand behind her like a guilty child.

"It's nothing."

He didn't argue. He simply reached around and took her right hand. "Which hand? This one? Did you get the sliver out?"

"Really, it's nothing."

He opened her clenched fist and critically inspected the small but ragged mark left by the sliver. "What did you dig it out with, a carving knife?"

"No, a needle." But it had been awkward probing at her right hand with the needle in her left, and the result wasn't exactly neat surgery.

"Why don't you have a bandage on it?"

"Now you sound like my mother!" Shar replied in exasperation. She tried to snatch her hand away, but he held it with unexpected tenacity.

Then he did something even more unexpected. He lifted her hand to his lips and gently kissed the small wound.

5

ASTONISHMENT MOMENTARILY PARALYZED Shar. His lips felt soft and warm, gentle as a whisper. But the shock that rocketed through her was more shout than whisper, an uproar of messages. "What are you *doing*?" she gasped.

"You accused me of acting like your mother. That's what my mother always did when I had a small hurt. It always worked, too." Solicitously he closed her fingers into a fist again. "Doesn't it feel better now?" The gold flecks gleamed mischievously from the rich depths of his eyes.

Shar just stared at him, unable to decide exactly how she did feel. Finally she shook her head helplessly, and a smile broke through the shock. Add unpredictable to the list of Tal O'Neal's personal assets. Or maybe it was a liability. At the moment she was too flustered to know.

"My mother always said a kiss was the best medicine. Maybe because when I was small it was probably the only medicine we could afford," he added, laughing a little ruefully.

"Yes. Well, I—I'm sure the finger will be just fine now."

"Good. I'll be in touch in a few days then, and we'll take a look at some of those other properties."

He strode jauntily from the room, and Shar slumped to her swivel chair. She opened her hand and looked at the finger he'd kissed, trying to decide if she should be angry or indignant. It was an outrageous thing to have done. Kissing an injured finger—right here in a professional office! Yet the brief episode struck her as more amusing than anything else. It wasn't as if he'd made some big passionate pass at her; kissing a hurt was the same kind of funny tender gesture he might have offered to seven-year-old Cindy.

Though Cindy, Shar reflected a bit guiltily, wouldn't have had that inappropriate flash of eroticism at the first touch of his lips. Uneasily she wondered if the reaction meant anything. It had been so swift, so unexpected, like the reflex to a tap on a knee. But it *didn't* mean anything, she decided firmly. At least nothing more than that she was young and healthy and that perhaps she was more passionate than she had cared to acknowledge these past few years.

SHAR MADE AN HONEST EFFORT to let that passionate nature take over on her date with Doug Morrison that evening. She wore a slinky silk Charmeuse dress, and Doug responded with extravagant compliments and a heady flow of champagne. She let him nuzzle her neck in the candlelit privacy of their dinner table, and she experimented with a nip on his earlobe. He reacted with an impassioned groan and whispered that she was driving him crazy with desire.

He drove her crazy, too. Unfortunately it wasn't with desire, and she quickly decided that the ear nip had been a drastic error. It had apparently aroused in him a voracious appetite for nibbling indiscriminately on any available part of her anatomy. Except *gnawing* was a more appropriate description, she decided with a grimace as he attacked the nape of her neck as if it were a succulent chicken leg.

Doug Morrison didn't spend the night in Shar's apartment. In fact he got no farther than the bottom of her steps, where she offered him profuse thanks for a marvelous dinner—and a no-nonsense handshake.

So much for Doug Morrison, she decided as she locked the door firmly behind her. Tal O'Neal had more sex appeal in his *knees* than Doug possessed in his entire body.

Though that was merely the opinion of an impartial observer, of course, not any indication of her personal feelings.

SHAR GOT OUT OF BED on Saturday morning feeling restless and out of sorts despite the gorgeous almost springlike weather. The only cloud in the sky was a plume trailing from the snowy summit of Mount Hood to the east. She had just one appointment scheduled, a nine o'clock meeting to show the Brewster property again. Always alert to possibilities, she had happened to mention it to one of the owners she had contacted about Tal's property. The client was frustratingly noncommittal after seeing the warehouse, saying he'd think about it. Afterward Shar went by to see Tripod. The kitten had a ready purr now, and its thin body already seemed to be filling out.

Then she felt at loose ends. She could go to the office, of course. Saturday was a good day to work the floor because people dropped by in response to newspaper ads and were attracted by a property featured on the firm's outdoor sign. Or she could go home and clean house.

Neither prospect appealed.

On impulse she decided she'd drive down to Medford and inspect the property Tal had for sale. She really needed a personal look at it to be able to give it a proper sales push. The realization that the drive would take five or six hours and that it was already past noon put a temporary damper on the impulse.

So she'd zip down on one of the frequent commuter flights that took no more than an hour. She'd done that before, though usually with more advance planning. She hurried home, telephoned the airline's ticket office, called her own office to get the address of Tal's Medford property and packed an overnight bag. An hour later, after a mad dash to make the flight, she was flying above the green and lush farmlands of the Willamette River Valley, delighting in a marvelous sense of freedom. For the first time in her many hours of flying she saw the lovely phenomenon known as a glory, a rainbow ring encircling the shadow of the plane on a thin layer of clouds below. She took it as a good omen.

She rented a car at Medford Airport, stopped briefly at a nearby motel to rent a room and then, using a map supplied by the car rental agency, drove to Tal's property. Along the way she noted that the location was excellent, in proximity to both railroad and freeway. The access road was in good condition, and properties in the area looked fairly prosperous and well maintained. So why hadn't his place sold, she wondered, feeling a surge of the energy that often came when she was confronted with a knotty problem. She had come down here mostly to get away from Portland temporarily, but now she was glad she was here.

She parked the car and inspected the property as a buyer might. Both lot and building were long and narrow, the front of the building only a few steps from the street. The building's construction looked solid, and the paint was in good shape. Two front windows were smashed, however, and one of the truck gates in the chain-link fence dangled from a broken hinge. When she slid out of the car she could see that in fact, all the windows along one side were broken. That seemed odd. She wouldn't have thought Tal was the kind of man to let property deteriorate.

She stepped through the angled opening between the fence and broken gate. Her booted feet crunched lightly on the gravel. She tried the door of the office area and found it locked. The broken windows were wide open, however, and after a moment's deliberation she brushed broken glass off the sill and crawled inside. At least this time she was prepared for exploration; she had on worn jeans and a blue nylon windbreaker.

Once inside, she picked her way across the litter of broken glass. A metal desk sprawled in one corner, broken legs awry. She was just peering at an electrical panel, which had also been smashed, when she heard a sound behind her. She whirled just as the door burst open and a broad-shouldered form filled the doorway.

"Okay, hold it where you are. I—Shar!" Tal's jaw literally dropped open, and his eyes widened in astonishment. "What are you doing here?"

"What are *you* doing here? You practically scared me to death." She leaned against the wall and closed her eyes for a moment, her heart thudding. "I thought you were supposed to go to a—" She broke off, only at the last moment remembering that she shouldn't know he was scheduled to attend a dinner with Nicole that evening. "And put down that . . . that weapon!"

He looked at the heavy tire iron in his hand as if he'd forgotten he was holding it. He smiled a little self-consciously and leaned the menacing length of metal against the doorjamb. "I drove up just in time to see someone disappear through the broken window. I thought it was one of the vandals, back for another assault on the place. But I guess it was you."

Vandals. Of course. That explained the broken windows and angled gate. Shar was glad she *wasn't* a vandal. Nice guy Tal O'Neal could apparently be one tough customer when the situation called for it. He had looked as if he would have used that tire iron if necessary.

"I got a call this morning that the place had been broken into and vandalized," he explained. "That's why I'm here. I came down right away to see how much damage had been done and get it repaired. But I sure didn't expect to find you here! You didn't mention anything yesterday about coming down."

"I told you that I like to personally inspect properties I'm trying to sell or trade. I just made a . . . last-minute decision to do it this weekend." She touched the pulse that still pounded in her temple.

"Are you all right?" He stepped closer and peered with concern at her slightly pale face. "I'm really sorry I frightened you."

"Sure. I'm fine." She brushed sweaty palms against her jeans. "I'm just glad you figured out it was *me* before you started swinging that chunk of metal!"

"Finger okay now, too?" He smiled with the same touch of mischief with which he'd kissed the small injury.

So he hadn't forgotten that incident, and memory of her confusing reaction did nothing to calm her generally shaky feelings. "Yes. It's fine."

"See? I told you."

"Yes." She tucked the hand behind her, half afraid he might do a repeat treatment. "Well, do you mind if I get on with my inspection of the property? That's what I came here for."

"Be my guest." He waved expansively toward the remainder of the building, then led the way to the shop area.

Shar felt self-conscious following him, somehow more aware of him than of the building she was supposed to be inspecting. His faded jeans clung to his lean hips and muscled thighs, drawing her eyes to the easy swing of his long stride and emphasizing the length of his legs. The denim jacket was taut over wide shoulders, loose at the waist. The turned-up collar brushed his dark hair and concealed what she had irrelevantly noted at the masquerade party was a kissable nape.

"The shop area could easily be either enlarged or made smaller, of course, by taking out that partition—"

He stopped to motion toward the partition, and Shar crashed into him. She backed off instantly, but not before she was all too aware of the solid male body beneath the denim. He turned to look back at her, and she flushed, embarrassed at having bumped into him, even more embarrassed by her own wayward thoughts. "Sorry," she murmured. "I was looking at the concrete floor," she improvised.

Looking at concrete, indeed, she scoffed at herself. She had been watching Tal's buttocks, like one of those leering women stuffing dollar bills in male bikinis at some strip show. Enough of *that*.

Briskly she said, "I don't believe our listing has the square footage of the building. Do you have the measurements?"

He didn't, so they went outside and she paced them off, removing her windbreaker in the pleasant warmth of the sunshine. Afterward she dug out her credit-card-size calculator and did a rough estimate of the square footage. He seemed impressed, but she shrugged off what she'd done. She had learned to improvise when a tape measure wasn't available.

They walked down the narrow lane beside the building and around the corner to the loading dock. "The dock looks rough, but it's solid," Tal said, "and there are gas and diesel pumps and underground tanks over there."

The lot next door was vacant, a forlorn tangle of tires and rusting car parts, blackberry bushes and piles of broken concrete and pipe. It was the only really junky-looking spot in the immediate area. Could that be why Tal's place hadn't sold? Possibly. The vacant lot was certainly an eyesore, possibly even a health hazard. Or it could be that the area's economy was too depressed at the moment to make a sale possible. Yet there was something about the layout of the property itself that struck her as not quite right. . . .

"You're not driving back to Portland tonight, are you?" Tal asked as they retraced their steps to the front of the building.

"Actually I didn't drive." She nodded toward the compact car parked outside the fence. "It's a rental car. I flew down."

"You're staying overnight then?"

"Yes."

"Then tonight I'm taking you to that dinner I owe you." His tone was decisive. "No arguments. The O'Neals always pay their debts."

"I can't go to dinner," Shar protested. "I didn't bring any clothes."

His gaze scanned her leggy jeans, cowl-necked sweater and high-heeled boots. He smiled when he said, "You look fine to me. I think you can manage to get by the No Shirt, No Shoes, No Service signs." Yet his expressive eyes said more than the offhand statement had, and his approval raised Shar's pulse far more than any of Doug Morrison's extravagant praise could have.

Well, she did have to eat, and she couldn't think of any good excuse not to have dinner with him. He obviously couldn't make it back to Portland in time for the dinner with Nicole, even if Shar declined his offer. And they might put the time to good use with a further discussion of his property.

Tal pushed back the cuff of his denim jacket and glanced at his watch. "I have to make some telephone calls and see if I can line up someone to repair the damage here. I'll pick you up about seven. Where are you staying?"

Shar hesitated. Having him pick her up at the motel would feel too much like a date. "Why don't I meet you somewhere?"

He gave her the name and address of a restaurant. After he had left she wandered around for a few minutes by herself, trying to decide what it was that gave her negative feelings about the property.

Once back in her motel room, she showered, put her jeans and sweater back on and went to meet Tal at the restaurant.

It was a family-type place, the kind of spot where the food was good and her clothes didn't make her feel out of place. Tal, evidently familiar with the menu, recommended the prime rib, and it was delicious. They started out talking about the vandalism at Tal's property, but somehow the conversation strayed and never did return to that subject. He'd been raised in the area and kept her amused with stories of his boyhood mishaps. They had blueberry pie for dessert, then more coffee. Shar wondered where Tal was staying but didn't want to ask.

There was only one awkward moment in the evening. It was just after they had walked out of the restaurant and were standing in the fresh-scented evening air under a starry sky.

Tal looked at his watch. "It's early yet." Vaguely he added, "Saturday night."

Shar could tell he was weighing something in his mind, and a mixture of anticipation and apprehension suddenly made her mouth go dry. Was he going to suggest something that would take this evening out of the business-acquaintances-who-just-happened-to-run-into-each-other classification? Nicole had said he was a terrific dancer....

But Shar would never know if he had had something in mind or what kind of dancer he was. Quickly she said, "Thanks for a lovely dinner. Your so-called debt to me has been more than repaid." She also made a point of looking at her watch. "And now I must get back to my room. I brought along some work to do."

He didn't question what she had to do, for which she was grateful, because the only work she had brought along was a manicure kit to do her nails.

"I'll be in touch," she called, turning from her car to wave. "Thanks again."

She did her nails and watched television in the motel room. She kept losing track of the movie's story line, even though it was a highly rated film that she had looked forward to seeing. Her thoughts kept straying to Tal. And Nicole. He must have been disappointed, having to come down here instead of going out with her. What was he doing tonight? No doubt he'd call Nicole. Would he mention that he had accidentally run into Shar? Probably not. No reason to. He had no idea that Shar and Nicole even knew each other. Much less, she thought, smiling a little ruefully, that they had subjected him to an outrageous seduction test.

She stayed up late but still slept restlessly. But the night wasn't entirely wasted, because by the time she stepped out of her morning shower she had figured out what was bothering her about Tal's property. She was just putting on bikini panties when the telephone rang.

She didn't remember having left a wake-up call, but perhaps she had. She lifted the receiver. "Yes?"

"Your breakfast is ordered. Be down at the coffee shop in ten minutes."

Tal hung up before she could protest. Of all the nerve, she thought indignantly. She could have been sleeping late . . . and not necessarily alone. How did he know— maybe she'd found an interesting male companion to enliven her trip.

On second thought, however, she realized she was starved. She dressed hurriedly and dashed down to the coffee shop.

Tal was watching for her and waved her over to a table overlooking the indoor swimming pool. "Did you go swimming last night?" he asked.

"No, but I should have, shouldn't I? It's gorgeous." A lush jungle of vines and trees surrounded the pool, and a waterfall cascaded over tiers of rock.

He stood up and gallantly held the chair for her, making her shake her head in bemusement. The man had ordered, not asked, her to have breakfast with him—but then treated her like a queen when she arrived.

"What am I having?"

"You'll see." He poured coffee for her from the gleaming pot on the small table, and she took an appreciative sip. Evidently he traveled almost as lightly as she did. He was wearing a fresh navy turtleneck this morning, but the faded jeans were the same. He looked rested, relaxed . . . and dynamically attractive.

"How did you know where I was staying?"

"I just called around until I found a place that admitted they had a redhead named Sharrel Hathaway on their guest list. Are you angry?"

"Actually I'm glad to have the chance to talk to you again. I think I've figured out at least one reason your property hasn't sold." She went on to explain her conclusions about the property having poor truck access to the loading dock.

"You could be right," he reflected. "I cussed that narrow truck lane and awkward turn for years, but it was something we had to live with, so I suppose I've never given much thought to how a buyer would see it."

"You may, of course, eventually be able to sell to someone who's willing to put up with it, but it would certainly increase the number of prospective buyers if good access was there. What I had in mind was that you might purchase that vacant lot next door. You could cut off enough footage to widen the access to the loading dock, clean up the remainder of the lot and probably resell it for nearly as much as you paid—" Shar broke off as their breakfasts arrived.

Hers was a huge waffle covered with mounds of strawberries and whipped cream, plus a bowl of sliced strawberries on the side. Before she realized what she was doing, Shar had dipped a finger into a creamy peak and stuck it in her mouth. The thick froth melted on her tongue, wickedly rich and heavenly luscious.

She savored the taste with half-closed eyes until she suddenly realized she was sitting there with the tip of her finger still in her mouth, and she smiled, feeling foolish. Decorously she picked up a fork to dip into the mountain of strawberries. Tal smiled, too, obviously delighted that his breakfast choice pleased her so much.

"How did you guess that strawberries and cream is my secret weakness?" The berries were almost as melt-in-the-mouth as the whipped cream, delectably sweet and juicy.

"You just look like a strawberries-and-cream person. I could tell from the way you dug into your prime rib last night that you're not one of those women who just pick at their food because they're always dieting."

"I'm embarrassed. I didn't realize my hearty appetite was so . . . obvious."

"Don't be. It's refreshing. You have no idea how little fun it is to take a woman to dinner and have her eat two lettuce leaves and a spoonful of cottage cheese."

Tal was also eating heartily, Shar noted. Ham, eggs, hash browns, biscuits, honey. And he was eyeing her strawberries.

"Would you like a bite?" she asked impulsively.

"Yes."

She scooped up a generous forkful of waffle, strawberries and whipped cream. She intended simply to hand it to him, but he used his hand to steady hers and took the bite directly off her fork. It was not the most graceful of procedures, and a bit of strawberry juice trickled down his chin. She reached across the table with a napkin and wiped it away.

"Somehow I feel Emily Post wouldn't approve of all this," she said with a laugh.

"This is our breakfast, not Emily Post's," he retorted. He released her hand almost reluctantly, then looked down at his plate. "Ham?" he suggested.

"Why not?" The bite of pink ham that he placed in her mouth was succulent, tender. And his biscuits and honey were quite tasty, too.

When the last strawberry was eaten, the last bit of rich whipped cream wiped up with the last chunk of waffle, Shar finally tried to return the breakfast to what it should be, a business conference. But Tal was having no part of that.

"No more shoptalk today," he ordered decisively. "I'm impressed with your astute observations about the property. I intend to follow through and investigate the possibilities of purchasing the lot. But not today. We both work much too long and too hard. Today is going to be different. I have everything planned. You ski, don't you?"

"I have a plane to catch at noon!"

"Don't you know the old saying? All work and no play makes Shar a dull girl."

"Am I a dull girl?" The dismayed question was out before she thought to stop it.

He studied her, head tilted thoughtfully. "No," he said finally. "No, you're not. You're a very beautiful, exciting and talented woman."

Shar's lips parted, their natural color emphasized by the stain of strawberry juice rather than by makeup, which she hadn't had time to apply.

Her eyes met his, and turbulent emotions churned through her. She quickly covered up with humor. "May I use that as a personal testimonial on my résumé?"

He stood up. "Use it however you wish." His tone was surprisingly brusque, as if her lighthearted question had angered him.

Just as well, Shar thought, half relieved, half regretful. Breakfast had turned into a disturbingly cozy event. She stood up, too. "I think I'll run back out to your property this morning—"

"I told you, no more shoptalk and no more work today. You'd better get your things out of your room because we won't get back from Mount Ashland before checkout time." He paused a moment, green-brown eyes narrowing, then added, "I'll come with you," as if he thought she might slip away if he let her out of his sight.

."This is crazy," Shar protested as he took her elbow and lightly but firmly propelled her toward the cashier's desk. She repeated her earlier statement about a plane to catch and added, "I don't have ski equipment—"

"You can change the plane reservation to a later flight or ride back to Portland with me. And there's rental equipment available on the mountain."

"I haven't been on skis in years!"

He demolished that objection, too. "If you once knew how to ski, you still do. You'll enjoy it."

Shar looked up at him indignantly. The macho man, always telling a woman what to do—and how to feel about it! But there was one thing *she* could do. She had her credit card out and on the counter while he was still reaching for his wallet.

"Hey, I don't invite a woman to breakfast and then let her pay!"

Shar didn't point out that he hadn't exactly invited her; he'd commanded her. "It's a perfectly legal business deduction for me," she pointed out. "Taking a client out for a meal to discuss business is still acceptable to the IRS." She signed her name on the slip the girl handed her.

"A business deduction!" Tal repeated. He sounded half insulted, half incredulous. She thought for a moment that he might even explode in anger, but what he finally did was laugh. "I guess I'm not accustomed to dealing with the liberated woman."

Shar was glad she'd paid the tab, even though Tal seemed a bit uncomfortable; it put them back on the level of business associates. Not that they had ever really slipped off it, of course.

He didn't back down on his decision to accompany her to her room, however. She had brought a minimal number of personal items in her overnight case, but it felt to

Shar as if they stood out like flashing red lights when Tal walked into the room: yesterday's lacy bra draped across the back of a chair, a bottle of spray perfume with a suggestive name splashed across it on the dressing table, bikini panties a cinnamon puddle on the floor. And her nightgown! She raced across the room and stuffed the jade froth into the overnight case.

Tal didn't pretend not to see. He just grinned. "Very nice," he said approvingly. Teasingly he added, "Matches your eyes."

There was also a certain amount of speculation in his voice, as if he wondered who was occasionally around to appreciate the seductive nightgown. Shar was halfway inclined to explain that no one was; she simply liked lingerie that felt sensuous and silky against her skin, even if she did sleep alone. And she'd bought the jade because she liked it, certainly not because it matched her eyes.

Shar hurriedly scooped up her toothbrush, makeup and manicure kit. She stuffed everything haphazardly into the overnight case. After fluffing a brush through her hair, she was ready to go. The entire procedure had taken ten minutes, which apparently impressed Tal.

"Most women take longer than that to get their make-up on," he observed.

Of course the comment wouldn't be based on hearsay. Tal might have exhibited nice-guy patience with Nicole's reluctance to enter into an intimate relationship, but he hadn't acquired that easy self-assured manner around women without having had some personal experience. He was far less uncomfortable being in this bedroom with her than she was having him there.

Though the situation might have been different if it had been his room and his bikini shorts draped over a chair for curious eyes to see, Shar thought defensively. Embarrassed, she snatched up the packed overnight case. What was she doing thinking about Tal O'Neal's shorts—bikini or otherwise?

She checked out at the main desk and paid her bill, then returned the rental car to the agency at the airport, Tal following in his car. She recognized the small sporty vehicle as the one she'd ridden in after the anniversary party. He suggested that she plan to ride back to Portland with him so that they wouldn't be tied to a certain flight time. That made sense, so Shar cancelled her plane reservation.

There was no snow on the valley floor and only patches of it beside the freeway until they reached the Mount Ashland turnoff. From there on the road was steep and winding, and the depth of the snow increased until they were driving through a white-walled canyon cut by snowplows. Open windswept stretches allowed occasional glimpses of the rugged mountainous country across the California line to the south and of Mount Shasta rising majestically above the lesser peaks.

There were few cars on the road, but the unpaved parking area near the lodge was jammed. Shar had to shade her eyes when she stepped out of the car. Sunlight on snow hit her eyes with dazzling brilliance, as if she had just stepped into the interior of a sparkling gem.

"I think we're going to wish we had sunglasses . . . and suntan lotion!" Shar exclaimed.

"There may be some in the glove compartment." Tal leaned into the passenger's side of the car and produced, not only a tube of suntan cream, but two pairs of dark glasses, as well. Shar spread a generous amount of cream on her face, and he put a careless dab on his nose and under his eyes. When she tried on the sunglasses, she got a small jolt. They were Nicole's; she was certain of it.

She felt uncomfortable for a moment, then quickly brushed away the feeling. She'd have to remember to tell Nicole what an unexpected convenience her sunglasses had been.

It took them some time to get out on the slopes. They had to buy a parking permit and take it back to the car. There was a line at the window to buy lift tickets, another line at the equipment-rental counter, and then it took more time to get boots that fit. Shar found herself becoming more excited and exhilarated all the time. The dazzling sunshine alone was enough to lift her spirits, and the air was invigoratingly crisp. Happy voices echoed from the slopes.

Finally they were clomping out with their rented equipment, Shar lifting her feet awkwardly in boots that felt large and unwieldy.

Tal laughed. "You'll get used to them again in a few minutes. How come you never go skiing back home? Mount Hood isn't far away."

"I guess I just don't take the time," Shar admitted. "It's faster to exercise by jogging near home or swimming at the health club I belong to. And sometimes all I have time for is a few calisthenics at home."

"You know what I said," he warned. "All work and no play—"

"Will make Shar a rich real estate agent someday," Shar finished, punctuating the tart rhyme by sticking out her tongue at him.

"Never try to give advice to a liberated woman," he grumbled. But he laughed and asked her which slope she wanted to run first. "That's the T-bar over there," he said, nodding in the general direction of a wide, fairly short slope. "It's rated an intermediate run. Beyond it, on the other side of those trees, you can see just a little of the

Windsor chair lift. And beyond that there's the Ariel chair that goes to the top of the mountain, if you're really good."

"Isn't there a nice bunny slope?" Shar asked doubtfully. "It really has been a *long* time since I've been on skis. I'd better start out on something easy. But you go ahead and use the chair lift," she added quickly. "Don't let me hold you back."

"Oh, no," he said, "I'm not going to miss this opportunity to give my expert advice to a liberated lady. We men have to maintain our feeling of superiority somehow, you know." He shook his head, looking bemused, and Shar knew he was remembering her credit card caper.

They put on their skis, and Tal led the way to the rope tow on the slope for beginners. Shar was glad she had happened to tuck a pair of gloves in her overnight case. She recalled that using a tow was a good way to get rope-burned hands.

Shar went down cautiously the first time, testing her balance and her control of the skis but also delighting in the almost forgotten thrill of sliding on packed snow and feeling the nip of the wind on her cheeks. Tal followed her, and at the bottom of the slope offered a little casual advice about her stance.

By the end of the fourth short run, with only one spill to mar her record, Shar felt confident enough to say gaily, "Okay, on to the next challenge. The T-bar?"

"Let's try the Poma first. It's a little more difficult than this slope but easier than the T-bar."

They skied down to the bottom of the Poma and waited in line for their turn. An attendant helped Shar catch the dangling rope and straddle the short bar, and she rode up the slope, her skis brushing the snow lightly.

There were trees on both sides of this steeper, narrower run. Tal went down first, his lithe supple body making the course look easy. He whipped to an expert stop and turn at the bottom, lifting his gaze to see Shar still poised at the top. She stood there apprehensively, conscious again of the long years since she had skied regularly. For an easy slope, this looked awfully steep! But Tal gave her an encouraging come-on motion, and she recklessly pushed off.

That run was truly exhilarating, without mishap, and so was the next, but on her third run, when she shoved off before Tal, something went wrong. She slipped, skidded sideways and wavered on one ski, as graceful as a tipsy giraffe, poles stabbing skyward. The skis came loose and merrily raced on without her, and then she was spinning and tumbling and sliding helplessly into the maze of trees.

Her first frantic dazed thoughts when she finally came to rest were *I've broken every bone in my body. I'll never walk again. And I'm blind. Blind! Maybe I'm even dead.*

At which point she realized she couldn't see because her face was ignominiously buried in a snowbank. She pulled it out and gasped for breath as she wiped snow from her eyes. Tal was beside her only a moment later. He brushed hair and more snow out of her face, his eyes dark with concern.

"Are you all right?"

"Am I alive?"

"I think so. You look alive." He touched her cheek with cold fingertips. "You feel alive."

She groaned. "And I'm sure no one could hurt this much if they weren't alive. Leave it to me to do something so dumb and clumsy."

"Everybody takes spills. Can you stand up? I think it's time we went over to the lodge for some lunch—unless you're really hurt...."

"Just my ego, I think. I was figuring I'd be ready for the Olympic trials next week."

He draped her right arm around his neck and put his left arm around her waist. Shar was reasonably certain she wasn't really injured, yet her legs felt rubbery and her body awkwardly heavy. She tried to stand, sagged, then heaved herself up with more determination.

It was too determined a heave. She knocked Tal off balance, and they both tumbled to the snow again, landing in a tangle of arms and legs and skis and poles.

"I'm sorry!" Shar gasped. They were twisted together like a lopsided X, Tal's skis making angled marks around them. "Are you all right? Did I hurt you? I'm sorry! How could anyone be so clumsy?" She looked at a denim-clad leg, uncertain if it was hers or his.

"It's okay. I'm fine." He rose up on one elbow and looked down at her. "But maybe you'd better postpone those Olympic trials for a few more days. A judge may . . . uh . . . frown on a contestant who bowls him over into the snow."

His lips twitched in a smile, and then he broke out laughing. After a moment's hesitation so did Shar.

"I have the feeling you could probably wipe out a whole *team* of judges," he added.

"I am sorry. Cancel the Olympic trials. You're all covered with snow." She brushed the clinging white crystals off his denim jacket.

"It's okay. Really." And still chuckling, he leaned over and touched her lips lightly with his in a small gesture of reassurance.

Shar didn't react for a moment. Her lips were too snow chilled to feel anything more than the light pressure of unexpected contact. She simply lay there, hair a wild red flame against the snow, surprised eyes open to evergreens and blue sky.

Then the warmth of his mouth spread to hers, and a flush stole over her cheeks and temples. She felt a sudden stillness in him as laughter ceased, and the only movement was the pounding of her own heart. He started to pull away, but some magnetic force seemed to hold their lips together—

And something happened.

His mouth never left hers. Instead, after a poised breathless moment, it came down harder and deeper, his casual gesture forgotten as something more basic took over. Her eyes drifted shut, snow-tipped lashes making glittering jewels of moisture against her flushed cheeks. He uttered a sound that she felt more than heard. She touched his jaw, half intending to push him away, but her icy fingertips thawed against the warmth of his cheek, and her hand crept around his neck, her fingers burying themselves in his dark hair. She felt as if she were drifting in some lush new world far from the cold snow and the pain of her bruised body.

His tongue made no move to penetrate the parted line of her lips, his body no move to slide over her. Yet the male power was there, like some ominous...or promising...shadow in the dark, hovering, waiting for release.

Waiting for a signal from her...or for the release of something within himself that held him back.

Like an irresistible tide, the heat flooded downward through her body, carrying with it a sweet awakening of desire....

6

"ANYONE HURT HERE?"

It was a member of the ever-alert ski patrol, his official insignia marked on his sleeve and cap. He was wearing mirrored sunglasses, and over Tal's shoulder, Shar caught her reflection in them...caught herself as he must see her, wantonly sprawled in the snow beneath Tal.

Tal jerked away, and Shar scrambled to a sitting position, thoroughly embarrassed. Out of the corner of her eye she could see that an incriminating flush marred even Tal's usual composure. Caught like a couple of adolescents fooling around in the snow!

"No, everything is fine. I just took a little spill. But I seem to have lost my skis." She stumbled to her feet, waving off the ski patroller's offer of assistance, and brushed snow from her jeans.

Tal was already on his feet, jamming his boots into the ski bindings, which had come loose when Shar knocked him over. "I'll go find them," he said with alacrity. He zoomed off, as if glad of the opportunity for escape.

Escape from the embarrassing scene, Shar wondered momentarily, or from her and the firestorm that had unexpectedly blazed between them? Because there was no doubt in her mind but that his reaction to the kiss had been as snow sizzling as her own, even though he had maintained control. Which was more than she could say for herself, she thought unhappily, remembering the delirium that had swept through her.

"Sure you're okay?"

"Yes. As soon as my. . . friend gets back with my skis, we'll take some time out and go over to the lodge."

"Good. Don't try to ski if you're feeling shaky."

The ski patroller glided away, and Shar was grateful that he hadn't thought it necessary to make some cute remark. She felt distinctly jittery about what had happened. A playful kiss on the finger to heal a small hurt was one thing; the kind of kiss Tal had given her here in the snow was something else indeed.

He returned with her skis, and she put them on by herself, bracing her hip against a tree so that she wouldn't need help. Right then she would have liked to have continued skiing to avoid looking at or talking to Tal, but she knew she would be courting real injury if she didn't wait until she was more steady on her feet.

They skied the short distance back to the lodge, locked their skis in a rack and went inside. The faintly steamy warmth, tinged with the not unpleasant scents of damp clothing and heated bodies, felt good. They stood in line for bowls of hot chili and coffee, then carried the food to a table by a window.

Shar kept up an uncharacteristic flurry of bright meaningless chatter. Didn't the coffee smell delicious? How late in the spring did the ski area stay open? Oh-oh, someone on the T-bar slope had just taken a nasty spill. This year's brilliant colors in ski outfits were so attractive. And even, in a desperate moment, what was the elevation here?

But in the back of her mind loomed another, much more ominous question: *If you're in love with Nicole, how come you're kissing me like that?*

And back came a disturbing question for her: how come she was reacting as if he'd lighted a flame in her that not even a flood could douse?

"Sure you're not hurt more than you're letting on?" Tal asked. "You sound a little nervous."

Nervous, yes. But not about a mere tumble in the snow. "No. I'm fine."

"You may not think so when you try to get out of bed tomorrow," he warned. "By the way, where did you learn to ski?"

Shar suddenly realized he wasn't going to make a big deal of the kiss and that she mustn't either. It was just one of those unfortunate things that occasionally happened between two people, a quick but essentially irrelevant spark. He hadn't, after all, done anything really deplorable, hadn't rammed his tongue into her mouth or lunged for her breast. And she hadn't done anything flagrantly foolish, either, she reminded herself, in spite of the way she'd felt.

She managed a bright smile and deliberately made her response arch and light. "You're granting that I actually learned to ski at some time?"

He laughed, and she thought she detected a note of relief. Had he been afraid she was going to insist on some dramatic confrontation about the implications of the kiss? "Really, where did you learn?"

Shar hesitated, not wanting the conversation to get too personal under the circumstances, but then realized this was a safe haven after all, because the answer didn't involve anything between them.

She told him about being raised in a suburb of Seattle, Washington, and skiing in the Mount Baker and Mount Rainier areas. He helped keep the conversation going, saying he'd like to get up that way for some hiking as well as skiing, and they talked around the neutral subjects of climbing Mount Rainier and hiking the Pacific Crest Trail.

After lunch Shar determinedly worked on reacquiring her old skiing skills. She declined Tal's occasional suggestions that they stop and rest, relentlessly driving herself up and down the slope, filling the afternoon with action that barred both conversation and thought. By midafternoon she felt confident enough to move up to the T-bar. She had hoped to progress to the Windsor chair lift, but she was satisfied when, after several tries, she finally made a respectable run down the intermediate slope. By then the pain of her fall was long forgotten, but she knew Tal's warning was correct; she'd pay for all this unfamiliar activity with aching muscles tomorrow.

Eventually they turned in their skis at the rental shop and headed back to the car. The sun was sinking now, casting long blue-tinted shadows chill with the feel of the coming mountain night.

"I didn't realize it was getting so late!" Shar exclaimed.

"That spill must have done you good," Tal observed as he opened the car door for her. "Your improvement on the slopes was quite dramatic. In fact, you raced around as if some kind of snow demon were after you."

Not a snow demon. A red-hot demon within herself— a demon from which she had to run because it kept wanting to relive those sweet moments sprawled in the snow with Tal, kept wanting to experience again the fiery taste and feel of him.

And that was unthinkable.

DURING THE LONG DRIVE back to Portland, they carried on a desultory conversation until full darkness closed around the small car and Shar drifted off to sleep. Tal woke her for a quick dinner stop in Eugene, after which she offered to drive. It was his turn to doze off then.

Shar was relieved. The kiss still lurked like a dangerous trap beneath their forced casual attitude, and she was afraid that sooner or later talk would make it loom to the surface. But without talk as a diversion, there was also nothing to inhibit her memory of the kiss. She savored its unexpected magic, trembled at the thought of magic that went beyond kisses.

Yet in spite of her own reaction and her strong suspicion that Tal had also been powerfully affected, Shar had to admire and respect the way he was handling the incident. He hadn't tried, as many men might have under the circumstances, to press for further intimacies, maybe by casually suggesting that it was late and maybe they should stop somewhere for the night. No, except for that one small . . . and no doubt regretted . . . slip, he had been admirably faithful to Nicole.

She glanced over at him as he slept in the reclining seat, head tipped to one side. In the faint glow of the dashboard lights he looked so appealing, and she battled an impulse to reach over and touch the dark fringe of his eyelashes to see if they felt as soft as they looked. His hands were lightly linked in his lap, and a shock of dark hair fell across his forehead. The angled light revealed the beginnings of a beard, a potent reminder of his masculinity. A nice man, she thought, not for the first time. Yet he was more, much more than that bland word implied. Handsome . . . forcefully masculine . . . exciting . . . fun . . . and faithful.

And he didn't snore, she thought with a rueful smile, remembering her earlier hopeful speculation.

Tal moved slightly then, straightening his head, and she quickly looked away, afraid he might catch her studying him in a way she really had no right to do.

When they filled the gas tank at Salem, Tal took the wheel again and drove on in to Portland. Shar's car was still at the airport parking lot, where she had left it when she had flown down to Medford. Tal suggested that she leave the car there until morning, and he'd take her directly home. Even though it was almost midnight and Shar was half-asleep again, she still had enough presence of mind to insist on going home alone in her own car.

At the airport she asked if he wanted her to investigate the possibility of buying the lot next to his Medford property. He said no, that he'd handle it himself.

"But I'll make it right with you financially," he assured her. "It was an excellent recommendation. It's just that I know the owner, and he's a little on the shady side. I think a little . . . uh . . . personal pressure about the possibility of going to the authorities and forcing him to clean up the lot may do wonders toward bringing the price down."

"Yes, perhaps so." He spoke in a pleasant, almost offhand manner, but Shar was reminded that she'd heard rumors of Tal's abilities as a ruthless negotiator. She didn't condemn a hard bargainer; shrewd bargaining was part of the real estate business. But she had the impression that he might enjoy exerting the pressure, and the thought was somehow disquieting after all the good things she'd been thinking about him. Tal had some tough facets to his character, no doubt about it.

He retrieved her overnight bag from the small trunk of his car and carried it to hers.

Mist swirled around the overhead lights in the parking lot, and she shivered in the damp chill. A little awkwardly, she turned to him. "Thanks for both the ride and the lovely day. I hope you don't have any more problems with vandalism."

"So do I, but if nothing else, it got me out of a dull, stuffy dinner I was supposed to attend. This was a lot more fun." He laughed lightly, as if having avoided the dull dinner was their friendly little conspiracy. With a small shock Shar realized it was the dinner with Nicole's friends that he'd been glad to escape. "I'll be in touch about taking a look at some of those other properties."

He made no move to touch her, gave no sign that anything unusual had happened between them that day. Yet at that very instant Shar made a decision. She could no longer continue to do business with him as a client; she must turn him over to someone else in the office. She owed it to both Nicole and herself. That spark had flashed between them once. It could again...perhaps with far more disastrous and incriminating results. It was even within the realm of possibility, Shar thought with a shiver that had nothing to do with the damp cold, that she might fall in love with him.

Tal was waiting to make certain her car would start. When it did he waved and disappeared into the foggy night.

THE VERY NEXT MORNING Shar made arrangements for Lex Anderson, one of the salesmen, to take over the firm's dealings with Tal, explaining briefly that there was a personality conflict between her and this client. Such a transfer wasn't a common happening in the office, but it had been done before. She told Lil to route any calls from Mr. O'Neal to Lex.

Also Shar called Nicole at noon, anxious to tell her that she had run into Tal in Medford so that there would be no possibility of the accidental meeting appearing underhanded or unethical. She explained about the skiing and the ride home, experimentally rotating a stiff shoulder as she did so. She wasn't as sore and aching as she had expected to be . . . but sore enough.

"Sometimes I think you're seeing more of Tal than I am!" Nicole wailed.

"Oh, I'm sure that isn't true!" Shar denied quickly. "But it just so happens that for . . . various reasons one of the other salesmen is going to handle him from now on. And besides, you see him almost every evening, don't you?"

"Did he mention me?" Nicole asked.

"Nikkie, I'm his—I mean I was his real estate agent, not his confidante."

Nicole sighed. "I know. It's just that he's seemed rather . . . oh, reserved lately, as if he's had something on his mind."

"I'm sure he does have a lot on his mind. The construction business is loaded with problems, everything from materials to labor to land-use laws. And then he had this vandalism thing come up—"

"Actually I'm glad to hear that you ran into him down there," Nicole admitted. "He told me he had to go down to Medford because the property had been vandalized, and I believed him of course, but I guess I'm relieved to know he was telling me the truth and that he wasn't sneaking around with some other woman."

Guilt momentarily surged through Shar. Should she tell Nicole about the kiss? No. It hadn't meant anything. No point in upsetting sensitive Nicole about something that was really no cause for worry. Quickly she told Nicole about her spill and knocking Tal down, exaggerating a bit for the sake of effect.

"You should have seen him zoom off to retrieve my runaway skis," she finished gaily. "I think he was afraid that if he got too close, my next attack on him might be fatal. I'm sure he'll be relieved to learn that someone else here at the office will be handling his real estate dealings from now on."

Nicole giggled, evidently delighted with Shar's whimsical version of the incident. "Sometime I'll have to ask him about his dangerous real estate agent."

"I think he'd probably prefer to forget the incident *and* me." Changing the subject, she asked, "What did you do about the dinner you and Tal were supposed to attend?"

"I went alone. It was buffet, so it wasn't as if Tal's not being there threw off some elaborate seating arrangement. It would have been more fun with him there, of course, but I enjoyed it, anyway. The artist was very interesting. Oh, I also happened to hear a surprising bit of information. Dave and Jill have split up."

"You mean they're getting a divorce?"

"Apparently they never got married. They were just living together."

Shar didn't offer any comments on Nicole's ex-husband. Nicole already knew how Shar felt about him. Until Tal came along, Shar had been afraid Nicole would never get over loving her first husband, in spite of what he had done to her.

"I'm buying one of the artist's paintings," Nicole added.

Shar wondered what Tal's reaction to the acquisition of a painting of a pale elongated female would be...but that wasn't her concern. Mostly she was simply relieved that Nicole wasn't upset by what had happened. Impressed, too, that Nicole had gone to the dinner alone. That was something her best friend certainly wouldn't have been able to do not so very long ago.

"Are you seeing Tal again soon?" Shar asked.

"He called a few minutes ago. He's coming over for dinner tomorrow night. Then we're going to the school for a little skit Cindy's class is putting on for a parent-teachers meeting."

More points for Tal. "That's good. Hang on to him, Nikkie. He's one of a kind."

Then Shar swallowed a foolish lump in her throat and briskly turned back to work.

IN MIDAFTERNOON the parcel arrived by delivery service. Lil brought it into Shar's office. Papers arriving by delivery were a common enough occurrence, but this oblong box didn't look like business papers. Shar stared uneasily at the carton. She was even more uneasy when she opened the brown outer packaging and found gift wrapping underneath. It was from Tal. She was sure of it, even though no identifying card was attached. Damn him! He had no right to send her gifts on the basis of one accidental kiss.

Furiously she ripped away the jade-colored wrapping. The choice of color was no accident, she thought angrily, remembering his comment about her nightgown matching her eyes. What was inside—expensive cologne? Or something even more intimate? She'd ship his unwanted gift right back to him and tell him exactly what she thought of a man who—

Sent a bottle of *liniment*?

Shar stared at the bottle in astonishment, and then anger dissipated into bubbles of laughter. Liniment! Leave it to Tal to come up with something like that. She opened the bottle and sniffed, blinking and fanning her nose at the strong aroma. And she had thought he was sending seductively scented cologne . . . with the presumption of personally sampling the scent on her body in some intimate setting. This was about as erotic as bad-tasting mouthwash! Again she had misjudged him.

She reached for the phone, eager to talk to him, thank him, laugh with him.

But she pulled her hand back without dialing. What Tal had done was sweet, funny, thoughtful. All the more reason why she mustn't call him, mustn't have anything more to do with him. An expensive gift with a built-in hint of amorous intent would have turned her off completely, but the improbable smelly liniment evoked a helpless melting feeling. Already he was tugging treacherously on her heartstrings; dangerous emotions were stirring. Falling in love was much more than a mere possibility.

She asked Lil to write Tal a polite note thanking him for the liniment and saying she was experiencing no ill effects from the fall.

SHAR SPENT THE EVENING at her health club, alternating between soaking in the hot tub and swimming easy laps in the pool. Back home she liberally applied the strong-scented liniment. The combined treatments were quite effective, and her joints and muscles were much more limber the following morning.

That afternoon after work she brought Tripod home.

The kitten inspected her new domain as a small arrogant princess might. She apparently considered her three-pawed status no more than a minor inconvenience as she leaped agilely from sofa to desk to stereo. Ignoring the padded bed Shar had prepared for her, she claimed an empty niche in the bookcase, regally settling between a stack of old multiple-listing books and a pasta cookbook that Shar had never gotten around to using. That soon became Tripod's second-choice sleeping area, however, because first choice was around the back of Shar's neck, wrapped around it, in fact. After the third evening Shar didn't know how she had ever gotten along without her furry neckpiece for company. The kitten also took to using the pet door that Shar had installed for old Slugger. Tripod was a true survivor, Shar decided affectionately—like her. Up from the ashes of ruin to success.

Shar heard only secondhand reports of Tal's activities over the next few days. From Nicole, she heard about dinners, a movie and some rose-pruning assistance—all the reports lace-edged and as dreamy as a Valentine message.

Shar was busy, too. She spent a day in the small pleasant town of Hood River, working on an exchange between an apple orchard owner and an apartment owner. She took Tripod back to the veterinarian for a checkup and some immunization shots. She worked out at the club. She called her mother in San Francisco and got a bubbly report of all the things she and her husband, Clyde, had been doing lately.

On the surface Shar's life was unchanged. Yet underneath she was all too aware that something was different. A restlessness stalked her days; dreams haunted her nights. Accomplishments at work dimmed and lost their former satisfying glow. She found herself turning down a lunch invitation with Nicole, reluctant to sit through another blissful account of Nicole's activities with Tal. She was also unhappily aware that all too many of her own hours, both waking and sleeping, were wound up in the same man.

The suspicion lingered in the back of her mind that she had done the one thing she shouldn't have; she had fallen in love with Tal. But she rejected the idea every time it arose, rationalizing his unyielding grip on her thoughts and dreams as merely logical, after all. At the moment there was no other attractive man to think about, so images of Tal rushed in to fill the vacuum.

The obvious solution was to find some other man to get so completely involved with that there was no room for Tal, but she found that wasn't an easy task. She talked and joked with men at her health club, but there were no sparks. She went to dinner with one of the men, anyway, and to a play with a former client. Both men were pleasant enough but as forgettable as last week's cold cereal.

Lex Anderson, the salesman who was now dealing with Tal, had a view of his client that was considerably less rosy than Nicole's.

Over a weekend, the only time Tal had available, Lex had taken Tal to see several of the properties in which he had earlier indicated an interest. Lex said that Tal barely glanced at the sites and found nothing favorable about any of them, that his attitude was hostile and critical and his temper bordered on the explosive.

"He acted as if he had a chip on his shoulder the whole time," Lex complained. "No wonder you shoved him off on me. He hinted not very subtly that he thought he was getting the runaround."

Shar doubted the problem was all with Tal. Lex sometimes had a grating know-it-all attitude, and he tended to bad-mouth any client who dared resist his heavy-handed salesmanship. None of that would sit well with Tal. Trying to be diplomatic, however, she just said, "I told you there was a personality conflict."

"That guy would have a personality conflict with a teddy bear," Lex muttered as he left Shar's office.

But that wasn't what Tal was really like at all, Shar protested silently. He was good-natured, fun, tender, generous—

Then she was annoyed with herself for defending Tal, even silently. Perhaps he was showing his true nature to Lex.

After another weekend passed, even Nicole hinted at a few undercurrents in her serene relationship with Tal. She confided that they had yet to make love, that something seemed to be holding them back. She was a little vague about who was holding back, and Shar had the impression both of them were.

The information surprised Shar, but it wasn't a subject she cared to discuss in detail, and she let the conversation drift elsewhere. Nicole herself seemed restless and moody, less talkative and bubbly than usual.

SHAR HAD JUST FINISHED SHOWERING and washing her hair one evening the following week when the phone rang. Tripod, who had a peculiar fascination for ringing telephones, ferociously leaped on the instrument. Shar laughed as she brushed the small playful creature away.

"Hello."

"You sound happy." And he sounded resentful.

Tal. Shar swallowed and yanked the pink towel more closely around her breasts. She thought about pretending she didn't recognize his voice or perhaps calling him Mr. O'Neal, but both actions seemed to place too much importance on the fact that he was calling her at home. Or that he was calling at all. "Tal? Is that you?"

"Yes."

"I was just laughing at Tripod—you remember the kitten I brought home? She likes to attack ringing telephones."

And towels, she added silently as the kitten landed on her hip and clung like a furry appliqué. The weight dragged the towel down, exposing one breast. Shar pulled the towel up again, then reached over to make sure the drapes were firmly closed so that she wasn't putting on a risqué performance for any passersby.

"I presume you've recovered from your skiing accident?"

"Yes . . . and thank you for the liniment. I believe Lil dropped you a note for me?"

For a moment, she thought he was going to demand to know why she hadn't thanked him herself, but he abruptly dropped the subject. "I hope you don't mind my calling you at home. These days there seems to be a problem getting past Lil to you at the office. It would almost appear that you've been avoiding me."

"Clients often call me at home." She didn't explain her unavailability at the office or acknowledge the accusation about avoiding him.

"But apparently you don't encourage home visits," he added.

Both her office and home phone numbers were listed on her business card. However, as Tal had obviously noted, her address wasn't listed in the telephone book. She didn't feel it necessary to explain that this was something single women often did as a security measure. She was doubly glad now that her address wasn't listed. She had the feeling Tal would have shown up unannounced at her door.

"Consultations in my home are usually not necessary," she agreed. She wanted to keep her voice coolly professional, but that was difficult with a kitten busily prowling her neck, curiously licking at the damp strands of hair and tickling bare skin. She cradled the phone on her shoulder, plopped the kitten firmly in the bathroom, closed the door... and lost her towel.

"What's so funny?" The husky voice was almost a growl. With sudden suspicion he asked, "Perhaps you're not alone?"

"I'm alone, except for a very mischievous kitten." She retrieved the towel and wrapped it firmly in place. She didn't feel comfortable talking to Tal in an undressed state, whether or not he knew that was her condition. "I've taken care of her now." She eased into her professional telephone voice. "Oh, I've been wondering...have you done anything yet about acquiring the lot next to your Medford property?"

"We're negotiating now."

"I'm sorry we haven't been able to come up with any trading prospects that appeal to you. Lex Anderson tells me that none of the ones you checked on the listing sheet were suitable after all."

"And what I want to know is why I'm all of a sudden shoved off on this Anderson character. I thought you were handling my listing."

"Well, I am, of course. We work together on these things. However, if there's a—" she hesitated, letting it sound as if she was deliberately being tactful "—personality conflict with Lex, I'll ask that someone else show you any properties that may interest you. And I'll be more closely involved, of course, if a trade materializes."

He wasn't about to be put off with polite evasions, however. Bluntly he asked, "What I want to know is why I'm no longer *your* client."

"I've been very busy—"

"So busy that you dumped all your clients off on someone else?"

No. Just the ones that I'm afraid I'm falling in love with. But all Shar did was laugh politely, as if she thought he was joking. There was a loaded silence, and she wondered if he was going to threaten to take his business to some other agency. She readied a polite acceptance speech for that decision.

However, as if he realized she was prepared to call his bluff, he said, "Okay, skip it. It doesn't matter. What I called about is this listing advertised by your company in last night's paper. 'Rustic vacation cabin on Oregon coast. Seclusion and superb ocean view.' I told you I might be interested in something like that. Why didn't you contact me about it?"

So he was just annoyed with her on a professional basis, Shar realized, relieved. It wasn't a personal call. She had almost jumped to a wrong conclusion . . . perhaps because when Tal was involved her thoughts weren't as firmly entrenched in business as they should be. And perhaps Lex was right about him. Tal certainly sounded ill-tempered at the moment.

"I'm sorry, but I'm not familiar with that particular listing, and perhaps I failed to indicate to Lex that coastal vacation property could be of interest to you—"

"Do you think you could *become* familiar with it?" he cut in with controlled sarcasm. "Surely there's something about it in that briefcase you carry around."

"If you'll excuse me for a moment, I'll check." Shar's tone was equally polite. She used the time to exchange the towel for a more secure, velour robe, deliberately not hurrying, then dug out the computer printout of new listings that she hadn't yet examined.

Damn Lex! He certainly should have contacted Tal about this, she thought as her gaze skimmed the listing. Details on the cabin itself were a little sketchy, other than that it was located on acreage in the Coos Bay area, but the owner had indicated a definite interest in using the property as a down payment on southern Oregon commercial or industrial property—possibly the ideal setup for Tal.

She relayed the information to him.

"Okay, sounds good. How do I see it?"

"Well, that could be a bit of a problem. Why don't I have Lex call you, and you can make arrangements with him?"

"I want *you* to show it to me."

"As I said, I'm very busy—"

"How about this weekend?"

"I can talk to Lex about that—"

"I told you, I want *you* to show me the property."

"Why are you being so insistent?" she shot back, angered by his stubbornness, panicky at the possibility of spending another day with him.

"Because . . . because it's your job, dammit. Everyone says you're the local genius at trading. Prove it to me."

The macho male, determined to run business *his* way, she thought scornfully, and not such a nice guy when crossed. But if he thought he could push *her* around, he was mistaken!

"I can't possibly make it this weekend." Her tone was cool and lofty, hinting at million-dollar transactions of higher priority. "Or next weekend, either," she added hastily to ward off any suggestions. And he couldn't make it during the week, she remembered. Lex had said the only time Tal had available now to look at property was on the weekend. "The only time I could possibly make it is—" she picked a day at random and tossed it out "—next Tuesday."

"Tuesday will be fine. Your car or mine?"

7

"BUT I THOUGHT—" Hastily Shar cut off her dismayed comment. "Actually, I—I doubt that we could drive down there, locate and inspect the cabin and make it back in one day," she said, playing for time.

"You're suggesting we stay overnight then?" His tone held a hint of challenge.

"No!" She absolutely was *not* suggesting they stay overnight. "The only way I could possibly fit the trip into my schedule would be to fly down and back the same day."

If she thought that would deter him, she was mistaken.

"Fine. I'll make the arrangements and let you know."

A fine mess she'd gotten herself into, Shar thought as she let an insulted Tripod out of the bathroom. The kitten haughtily withdrew to her niche in the bookcase.

Shar blow-dried her hair and wondered what to do now. She supposed she should tell Nicole about the appointment with Tal, yet was that really necessary? She was beginning to feel uncomfortably like a tattletale of sorts. Tal was, after all, a client, and this was just a business matter. Perhaps he would even cancel before next Tuesday. But she doubted that. He had sounded as if his mind was made up. Could she send Lex in her place at the last minute?

The thought of the possible repercussions if she tried that trick made her shudder lightly. Tal would never stand for it.

TAL WASN'T IN THE AIRPORT WAITING ROOM when Shar arrived on Tuesday morning. She was surprised because she had taken care to arrive at almost the last minute herself. Had he changed his mind or forgotten the trip? She was balancing relief with an unwanted twinge of disappointment when he hurried in. He picked up boarding passes before coming over to where she was sitting. They had no luggage to check, of course.

"Sorry. Some last-minute complications took longer than I expected." He had a distracted air, no doubt preoccupied by business problems, which gave Shar a perverse bit of satisfaction. If he hadn't insisted that she show him the coast cabin, he'd be where he should be today, taking care of those business problems. "I've arranged for a rental car at the airport for when we arrive."

"I'd like to return on the two-forty-five flight, if at all possible." Shar had checked the flight times herself, even though Tal had made the arrangements. "There's only one flight back to Portland after that, at five-thirty-five."

If he heard, he gave no sign of it. "Miserable weather," he muttered. He sounded as if the cold blowing rain was a personal affront . . . something that she, perhaps, had concocted to annoy him.

They had only a few minutes to wait before boarding the eighteen-passenger plane. Their seats were across the aisle from each other, which was fine with Shar because it made conversation inconvenient. Tal didn't appear inclined to talk, anyway. He obviously had problems on his mind, but he had too much self-control to let more than a faint scowl and the compression of his firm mouth give him away.

The weather was indeed miserable. Shar was made uncomfortable by the gray-white fog pressing against the windows of the plane, although the trip wasn't actually rough. She wondered if there might be problems landing, but the experienced pilot handled that neatly.

They picked up the rental car just outside the doors of the small terminal building. Tal drove. The weather was even worse than it had been in Portland. The furious swishing of the small windshield wipers barely kept pace with the downpour.

"The cabin is in something called the Seven Devils area," she said, tilting the paper to catch the gray light.

"Sounds promising," he grumbled. He dodged a water-filled pothole. "I wonder where that name came from."

The comment seemed to be no more than a reflection of his ill temper, and Shar didn't respond. She wasn't familiar with the area and had only the directions on the listing to go by, which were none too clear. They got lost and wound up on a muddy road that dead-ended at a dismal pile of timber slash left over from some old logging operation.

They backtracked to Coos Bay. By then it was well past noon, so they stopped for hamburgers and coffee at a cheerful, cozy restaurant. The waitress helped them decipher the directions to the cabin. Tal had very little to say. Shar suspected he was sorry he had insisted on this ridiculous trip but his male ego wouldn't let him admit it. Tal paid the check, the hard line of his mouth warning her that she'd better not whip out her credit card.

They followed the waitress's directions, crossing a drawbridge and turning south on a paved road. After a few miles the scattered houses became even sparser, and then another turnoff took them down a steeply winding gravel road. The isolated area had a wild tangled beauty in spite of the gray curtain of rain, with dark forest so dense that it looked almost impenetrable, banks of lush ferns, mounds of incongruously cheerful Scotch broom heavy with yellow blooms.

They found the driveway, and Tal got out to open the wooden gate. He was wearing tan slacks and the translucent plastic raincoat with the small familiar rip. He walked down the overgrown driveway, apparently to check it out, before returning to the car. Surprisingly, when he came back, his mood seemed to have lifted, as if the rain-washed air and his few moments alone had cleared the nagging problems from his mind.

"Beautiful setting," he offered. "You can hear the ocean from here. Sounds pretty wild."

"Did you see the cabin?"

"No, I didn't go that far."

The rain had let up, but moisture hung palpably in the air. Drooping branches brushed the car from above and wet grass swished underneath as Tal guided the car carefully down the narrow, puddled lane. A final turn deposited them almost at the doorstep of the small A-frame cabin nestled beneath a towering fir and flanked by a profusion of Scotch broom. Beyond the cabin the world seemed to end in a bank of gray mist, but from the mist came the massive roar of the storm-swept ocean.

Shar instantly fell in love with the rustic cabin, the forested setting, the angry sea. Never mind that it was isolated, that the cabin roof needed repair and that some small creature had built a nest of sticks and twigs in a corner of the porch. The wild, fresh scents of sea and forest invigorated her. The roar of the surf quickened her heartbeat and danced in her blood. The thrust of the wind swept the cobwebs and worry away. On city streets rain was dreary and depressing, something to escape as quickly as possible. But here she longed to race to the beach and delight in the savage display of the elements, to become one with them. If Tal didn't get the cabin in a trade, she just might see if she could swing the purchase price herself!

She found the key where the listing said it had been left, dangling from a nail hidden under the porch railing. She handed it to Tal and left him standing on the porch while she dashed to the edge of the bluff, not bothering with the umbrella, leaving her red-gold hair streaming bannerlike in the wind. Some ten or fifteen feet below, silvered driftwood jammed the bank, the seaward edges of old logs and stumps lifting and falling with the primitive beat of the attacking sea. And out of the gray mist beyond the driftwood, moving mountains of white fury rose like foaming specters from some other world, wave following wave in massive assault, each retreat swallowed up in the next onslaught. Shar closed her eyes and lifted her face, letting the mist of sea and rain bead her skin with cold jewels of moisture. She felt as if she had stepped into another world, a world where she was no longer earthbound, where she could as easily dance on the sea as walk on solid land, where drops of rain were falling diamonds.

She instinctively took a step backward when the sea, like some careless god playing with a lance, lifted a twenty-foot log and tossed it against the bank. She didn't realize Tal was behind her until he caught her lightly, his hands on her upper arms. She glanced back over her shoulder at him, her pulse suddenly pounding to a different stimulation.

"You look like a goddess out of mythology, standing there with your hair blowing like a red flame in the mists." He was looking at her, not the swirling tempest of water and foam and driftwood below. His voice held a rough tender huskiness. His grip tightened, as if he thought she might grow as insubstantial as the mists, leaving him with nothing but emptiness between his hands.

The wind shifted, billowing the banner of her hair into his face. Instead of retreating from it, he buried his face in the flowing mass, letting it tangle with the darkness of his own hair, glorying in the caress of silken strands on his cheeks. Then he turned her to him—

No, no, no, he *wasn't* doing that, Shar thought wildly. Her imagination was running away with her, fantasy overwhelming reality—all these thoughts of mystical sea gods with lances and mythical goddesses with hair of flame. Perhaps she had even imagined that Tal had said that.

She broke away, gathering her hair into a ponytail to tame it, breaking contact with the mesmerizing gold flecks of his eyes, clutching at reality.

"Well, we'd better take a look at the cabin before... before we run out of time, hadn't we?" she said, trying to shake off that strange, other-world feeling that had enveloped her for a moment. She glanced at her watch as they walked back toward the cabin, wiping the glass face to clear it because the numbers seemed to float instead of lying there solidly as they should. They had already missed the two-forty-five flight, she realized.

"Shar..."

She hastened her steps, afraid of something she heard in his voice. More afraid because she knew she *wanted* to hear something. "We'll have to rush to get back to the airport by five-thirty-five."

He unlocked the cabin, stepping inside ahead of her, as if there might be dangers to ward off. Shar fell in love with the rustic interior, too. The main floor was all one room, only a scarred plank counter separating kitchen from living room. The rock fireplace rose to the roof along the far wall, with windows on either side. Tal tried the light switch, but nothing happened. Shar pulled back a rough burlap drape to let light in. It revealed worn spots on the flowered sofa and chair. And from somewhere came the steady plop-plop of water through a leak in the roof. Shar didn't mind. She could handle a hammer and nails.

Pressing her fingertips together, she dreamily pictured herself curled up on one of those worn spots with a good book, a cup of spiced wine in hand, a cheery fire crackling and popping beside her. Tripod would love it, too! All the scene needed was—

She broke off that thought before the hazy image of a familiar masculine frame could take solid shape.

There was a cozy loft above the kitchen to sleep in, with the slanted roof angling over the bed. The soft old mattress buried her fingertips when she touched it. The rain had started again and drummed musically against the weathered shake roof.

Then Shar realized that Tal was once more looking at her, not at the surroundings. She also realized that Nicole would probably be far less enchanted with the cabin than she was. It was too isolated, too primitive. Nicole's idea of rustic was open beams over a redwood hot tub, not unfinished woodwork and open shelves for cupboards. Shar wasn't even certain this place had indoor plumbing, but a moment later she found a tiny bathroom off the kitchen. Nothing happened when she turned the water faucet, however.

"There's probably a private well, and the pump won't be working if the electricity's shut off," Tal said. "What do you think of the place?" His faint smile said he suspected he already knew.

"What I think really isn't important," Shar answered, determinedly aloof and neutral. Professional ethics required that she give him first chance at the property, and not try to buy it out from under him. She added her standard line for showing a property riddled with flaws. "It has a lot of possibilities."

"You don't sound as if you're trying very hard to sell it to me." The comment was mild, but she sensed a challenge behind it.

"I'm not a hard-sell type of salesperson. But if you're interested in making a trade, I'll try to arrange it for you."

"I'll think about it."

"Good. Then if you've seen enough, we should be going."

He didn't move, just stood there looking at her with a faintly speculative expression. She avoided his eyes, suddenly anxious to get outside, to return to the impersonal safety of the airport and the plane. In the confines of the small kitchen she was too aware of Tal as a man, not a client. Too conscious of everything male about him: the solid span of his shoulders, the taut muscles of his thighs. Too aware of his masculine aura of vitality that seemed to reach out and wrench something deep inside her.

Her heartbeat was too loud, her breasts too taut, her mouth too dry. She kept remembering the kiss they'd shared, wondering if he was thinking of it, too. She felt as if she were caught in a dangerous force field, as if powerful currents were circling in predatory patterns around them.

She turned and fled, not bothering to invent an explanation, leaving him to close the drape and lock the door. She huddled in the cold car, damning herself for feeling this way, damning him for dragging her there.

"We'll have to hurry," she said tightly when he slid into the car. Winter's short daylight was already fading, hastened by the increasing intensity of the storm. She could barely make out the numbers on her watch. "It's already after four o'clock. The plane leaves at five-thirty-five."

"I believe you've mentioned that a time or two already."

He put the gearshift in neutral and turned the key. Nothing happened. He frowned, pumped the accelerator a few times and tried again. Still nothing happened.

"What's wrong?"

"I don't know. I'll have to check."

He fumbled underneath the dashboard until he found the latch that opened the hood. Now falling rain and on-coming darkness blotted out even the edge of the bluff overlooking the sea. He hesitated a moment, then turned up the collar of his rain jacket and opened the car door.

His head and shoulders disappeared under the open hood. Rain pounded the unprotected lower half of his body, leaving dark spots and streaks on his tan slacks. He moved around to the other side of the car, and she couldn't see him at all. Frustrating minutes inched by. Shar worried about making the flight and felt guilty about sitting here in the dry car while he got soaking wet.

Finally she opened the car door. "Can I do anything to help?"

"Got a flashlight? It's getting so dark I can't see a damn thing." Water drizzled across his face and dripped from his dark hair.

Shar handed him the penlight she always carried in her purse. She got out and peered under the hood with him.

"Get back inside. You can't do anything."

"But you're getting soaking wet."

"No point in both of us getting that way."

She got back in the car, and a few minutes later he slid behind the wheel and tried the ignition again. Again nothing happened.

"Couldn't we . . . push it or something to get the engine started?" Shar's knowledge of disabled cars was definitely limited.

"Push it where? In case you haven't noticed, the car is pointed toward the ocean."

"Oh." Shar's voice was small, chagrined.

"I'd say that, barring an unexpected rescue by the cavalry, we're stuck here for the night. Maybe in the daylight, if the rain ever lets up, I can figure out what's wrong."

"We can't stay here overnight!"

"You have a better suggestion?"

"We'll . . ." Shar searched frantically for some solution. They *couldn't* stay here together overnight. She didn't stop to examine the dangers in explicit detail; she only knew they were there. Explosive dangers of the flesh, even deeper dangers of the heart. "We'll walk out and get help."

"Don't be ridiculous. We're miles from help. It's almost dark, pouring down rain—"

"I don't care! I'm going to walk out."

"That's foolish. Even if we managed to get back to town, we couldn't get a plane out until tomorrow. We can be perfectly safe and reasonably comfortable here for the night."

Safe? Comfortable? Shar had a sudden image of dancing flames in the fireplace, the two of them together beside it, a long intimate night ahead of them. It was a sinfully tempting image, one she had to battle not to succumb to without protest. Abruptly she flung the car door open and slid out. Solid sheets of rain instantly slammed against her face, but she doggedly ducked her head and started up the lane.

Tal was out of the car, yelling at her angrily, "Hey, come back here! I'm not going to let you do that!"

He grabbed her arm, and she yanked away. "You have nothing to say about what I do!"

"The hell I don't!"

He reached for her again, but she dodged his grasp. A wet branch struck her in the face. She brushed it aside and blindly stumbled on, high-heeled boots slipping on the muddy lane as she tossed glances at him over her shoulder.

"Hey, watch out! There's a puddle! You're going to—" The next minute he was looking down at her mud-splattered face. Wryly he finished the warning. "Fall."

Shar slowly sat up. She was in four inches of cold muddy water, her back wet from shoulders to heels, her front splattered with brown splotches. She raised one hand, started to brush rain and mud and hair out of her face, then realized her hand was covered with mud. She blinked back tears. There was nothing to cry about, dammit! She wasn't hurt, just wet and cold and dirty. . . and humiliated and angry. And helpless. The tears ran down her cheeks, blending with rain and muddy splotches.

"Okay, enough independent, liberated-lady stuff. We're staying here tonight."

"No! I—I'm not moving!"

He didn't argue with that obviously implausible statement. He merely slipped one arm around her shoulders, the other under her knees, and lifted her out of the puddle. Shar battled tears.

"Put me in the car," she demanded.

"No. We're going into the cabin. We're going to build a fire and see if we can find anything to eat, and then we're going to get a reasonably comfortable night's sleep."

Two people. One bed. "How?" she demanded.

"We'll figure that out when the times comes."

Suddenly Shar was pounding him on the chest and shoulders with her fists, anger and frustration bursting out in a barrage of blows. "You did this on purpose, didn't you?" She paused only long enough to wipe wet hair out of her eyes before attacking him again. "You deliberately did something to—to sabotage the car!"

Tal paused at the porch steps. "Why would I do that?" His calm reasonable tone contrasted sharply with her panic, and her blows on his chest went as unheeded as the raindrops.

He set her on her feet under the shelter of the porch roof. She swallowed and blinked, her perspective suddenly righting itself. Yes, why would he do that? He was in love with Nicole, his faithfulness tested and proven. It was only she who wasn't to be trusted, she whose thoughts roamed in wicked directions. "I—I'm sorry," she apologized lamely. She had to get hold of herself.

He unlocked the door and pushed it open for her. When she didn't move he gave her a firm shove through the opening. "Yank one of those drapes down and wrap up in it while I find something to start a fire."

He found dry wood in a shed behind the cabin and within moments had a crackling fire going. The flames were bright and cheerful, but the semicircle of heat extended only a few feet from the fireplace. Shar stayed on the sofa, huddled under the brown burlap drape, warmed enough to keep her teeth from chattering but still soggy and uncomfortable.

Tal went to the shed and returned with another armload of wood. "You'd be more comfortable if you took off your clothes and hung them to dry in front of the fire."

"I'm fine."

He shrugged. "Suit yourself."

"I don't see *you* taking off your wet clothes and drying them by the fire."

"I'm not as wet as you are," he pointed out reasonably. "However, if it would make you feel more comfortable . . ." He started unfastening his belt, his eyes on hers, glittering with bold challenge.

Warily Shar tightened the burlap drape, suspecting he was teasing her but not inclined to test him. "Don't bother."

He grinned and refastened his belt, making her feel foolish. With as much dignity as possible she went to the tiny cold bathroom and removed her pants and blouse. And then her bra and panties, as well, because she was soaked to the skin. There were some ragged towels folded on a shelf above the sink, and she dried her body.

A knock sounded on the door. "I got a pan of rainwater out of a barrel out back. Want it?"

"Yes." She stood behind the door and reached around to accept the pan of water. The water felt almost icy when she dipped a towel into it to wash the mud splatters from her face, but it was clean and welcome.

She tried several arrangements of the burlap drape, anger and frustration finally yielding to reluctant amusement as she considered her predicament. At home she had a closet full of expensive tailored clothes—a wardrobe designed to promote the image of a competent, professional businesswoman. And here she was, trying to decide how to wear a brown burlap drape.

She finally settled on sarong style, tucking the ends in at the top and adding a strip of towel at the waist for security. When she stepped out of the bathroom she was surprised by a tantalizing aroma rising from a pan at the edge of the fire.

"Found a can of chili under the sink," Tal explained. "And—would you believe it—wine!"

He produced the bottle with a flourish. The dollar-twenty-nine price tag was plainly visible. In spite of wanting to be serious and reserved, Shar felt a giggle coming on. Canned chili, cheap wine, burlap drape, leaky roof...

And the most attractive man she'd ever met. But she quickly brushed that thought aside. "There's nothing like a fine wine to pull a meal together," she agreed.

"I found one old spoon but no bowls or glasses, so we have to share," he warned.

"I don't mind."

He gave her an odd thoughtful look. "Neither do I."

She spread her clothing to dry on a hard-backed wooden chair, discreetly putting her lacy underthings on a rung beneath the seat so they wouldn't be in plain sight. She sat on the sofa with her legs decorously tucked under her. He pulled the flowered chair up close so that they could both eat out of the pan and drink from the wine bottle. The wine tasted more like a soft drink than an alcoholic beverage, but under the circumstances Shar wouldn't have traded it for the most expensive vintage.

Once, when she had the spoon, she felt him studying her. "You know, for a beautiful sophisticated lady, you're kind of a klutz," he remarked not unkindly.

"Thanks. I needed that."

"A fall on the ski slope, a tumble in a muddy puddle..."

To say nothing of spilling a drink on herself at a certain anniversary party, she thought wryly. She was halfway inclined to tell him about that night, until he spoke again, softly.

LAST CHANCE TO WIN A FABULOUS PRIZE

TELL US WHERE YOU'D LIKE TO GO

WIN
an Island-in-the-Sun VACATION for 2

Here's special thanks for your interest in HARLEQUIN TEMPTA-TION love stories—and our special way of calling attention to the exciting, no-strings-attached Preview Service offer on the other side.

Win a fabulous, expense-paid Island in the Sun vacation for two to your choice of beautiful BERMUDA, sunny ST. THOMAS, or incredible ACAPULCO. All vacations are for a full week…and we will tell you on your birthday if you win. See next page.

BONUS:
another 101 winners

Simply write the month & date of your birth on the return card, next page, and you may win one of our bonus prizes—a lovely collection of exotic & intriguing perfumes, direct from France.

Win "Instantly" right now in another way
...try our *Preview Service*

Get 4 FREE full-length Harlequin Temptation books

Plus this elegant jewelry bag

Plus a surprise free gift

Plus lots more!

Our love stories are popular everywhere...and WE'RE CELE-BRATING with free birthday prizes—free gifts—and a fabulous no-strings offer.

Simply try our Preview Service. With your trial, you get SNEAK PREVIEW RIGHTS to four new HARLEQUIN TEMPTATION novels a month—months before they are in stores—with 11%-OFF retail on any books you keep (just $1.99 each)—and Free Home Delivery besides.

THERE IS NO CATCH. You're not required to buy a single book, ever. You may even cancel Preview Service privileges anytime, if you want. The free gifts are yours anyway, as tokens of our appreciation.

It's a super sweet deal if ever there was one. Try us and see.

LAST CHANCE EXTRA! Sign up for Preview Service now, get lots of free gifts *AND* automatically qualify to WIN THIS AND *ALL* 1986 "Super Celebration" PRIZES & PRIZE FEATURES. It's a fabulous bonanza—*don't miss it!*

IMPORTANT

Stick this "Sun" seal on return card

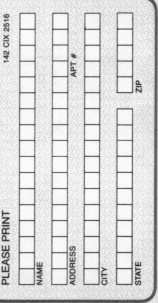

only if signing up for Preview Service.

Otherwise, mail card without. Your chances of winning this month's featured prizes are equally good either way.

PRINTED IN U.S.A.

HARLEQUIN TEMPTATION

FREE GIFTS—FREE PRIZES

YES I'll try the Harlequin Preview Service under the terms specified herein. Send me 4 free books and all the other FREE GIFTS. I understand that I also automatically qualify for ALL "Super Celebration" prizes and prize features advertised in 1986. I have written my birthday below. Tell me on my birthday what I win.

WIN A GREAT PRIZE

◄ If you are NOT signing up for Preview Service, DO NOT use seal. You can win anyway.

FILL IN BIRTHDAY INFORMATION BELOW

MONTH   DATE

this month's featured prizes—a fabulous Island in the Sun vacation for 2 + as an added bonus for 101 lucky entrants, exotic & delightful Perfume Collections, direct from France.

PLEASE PRINT   142 CIX 2516

NAME

ADDRESS   APT #

CITY   ZIP

STATE   ZIP

PLEASE PICK VACATION SPOT YOU PREFER ☐ BERMUDA ☐ ST. THOMAS
☐ ACAPULCO. Gift offer limited to new subscribers, one per household, and terms and prices subject to change.

IMPORTANT REMINDER:
Use "Sun" seal ONLY if you are signing up for Preview Service & want a chance to win this and all 1986 "Super Celebration" Sweepstakes prizes & prize features. Otherwise, mail card without seal.

If card is missing write
**Harlequin
"Super Celebration"
Sweepstakes**
901 Fuhrmann Blvd.
P.O. Box 1867
Buffalo, NY
14240-1867

Harlequin
"Super Celebration" Sweepstakes
901 Fuhrmann Blvd.
P.O. Box 1867
Buffalo, NY 14240-1867

PLACE
1ST CLASS
STAMP
HERE

"I find something about a softhearted, beautiful, sophisticated klutz very appealing."

She handed him the spoon, but he didn't seem to notice, and it clattered into the almost empty pan.

"Why have you been avoiding me?" he demanded.

"I've been busy—"

"That isn't why." He pushed the pan aside and moved onto the sofa beside her. He braced an arm behind her. "Tell me the real reason."

"You're . . . imagining things." She picked uneasily at a loose burlap thread.

"I wasn't imagining the way you reacted when I kissed you on the ski slope. And I damn sure wasn't imagining how *I* felt at the time."

There was no point in denying her reaction that day; it had obviously been too apparent. But she refused to explore his reaction to the kiss. "People make mistakes, and sometimes things like that . . . just happen."

"So it would never happen again."

"No. . . ."

His fingertips touched her cheek and traced the fragile but stubborn line of her jaw. Firelight played over the golden flecks in his eyes, caught the angles of his cheekbones, gleamed on his still-damp hair. His expression was faintly brooding, even a little resentful.

"Who are you, Sharrel Hathaway? Sometimes I think I know all about you. You're just another clever ambitious businesswoman. And then you turn all soft and mysterious on me, and I think maybe I knew you in another time or place, another world . . . and that's why I can't get you out of my thoughts, even when—"

He didn't finish what he'd started to say. His lips came down on hers, hard and hungry and demanding, as though the act of speaking had been ambushed by deeper more urgent forces.

Shar's senses swirled and reeled, as if she'd been struck on the head. But it wasn't pain she felt, not pain at all. It was a sweet fire, a heady intoxication, a tantalizing weakness.

She tried to draw back from the kiss, tried to strengthen her resolve, which was becoming as insubstantial as the banks of mist over the sea. Nicole. She raised the name, held it as a flaming placard of defense in her mind. Nicole, Nicole, Nicole! Nicole was her best friend. Nicole was in love with Tal. She owed Nicole her friendship, her help, her loyalty.

And yet it was all slipping away from her, the name fading out of existence, lost in the tumult of more urgent messages from her senses, drowning under the bursting dam of her own held-back emotions.

This kiss had none of the restraint of that kiss on the ski slope. His lips roamed hers with abandon, exploring, teasing, demanding, urging. His tongue entered her mouth, filled it, withdrew. Entered again, differently this time, delicately, questioningly, changing from the first raw demand of passion to a flirty dance of temptation.

Temptation that Shar couldn't resist. The tip of her tongue met his and followed its tantalizing retreat into the sweet warmth of his mouth. He tasted of the wine, smelled of the rain and the outdoors. And then his tongue came back to meet hers, to make her give a small moan of pleasure and desire. His hand was on the nape of her neck, fingers tangled in her hair. She felt the throb of her pulse in her throat, and as the kiss continued, fiery and sweet, rough and tender, the throb grew larger and larger until it threatened to engulf her.

"You see?" he whispered when he finally withdrew his mouth from hers a fraction of an inch. "The other time wasn't an accident, wasn't one of those things that 'just happen.' It happened again. And I've been aching to kiss you again ever since the day we went to Mount Ashland." His hand slid to her bare shoulder, cupping and squeezing the firelit skin, shooting electric darts deep into her.

He touched the tip of his tongue to the edge of her lower lip, ran it back and forth along the moist opening until she shivered with the tension of mounting desire. And then he drew back, misinterpreting the small shiver. She made a small sound of dismay at the loss, but he misinterpreted that, too.

"But I don't suppose you came here with the idea of having me make love to you." The comment held more frustration than anger. His hand moved back to her throat, his expression faintly brooding again.

No, Shar thought tremulously, she hadn't come here to make love with him . . . but she'd already made passionate love with him in a dozen disturbing dreams, and the temptation to turn those dreams into reality flowed through her veins like a drug. "Why . . . why did you want to come here, Tal?"

"Because I wanted to see you. Because I couldn't get you out of my mind. Because you were avoiding me."

She swallowed, let out a held breath. "You were just piqued because I shifted you to Lex. Your male ego was punctured." She touched his chin with a fingertip, partly to keep his mouth from dipping to hers again, partly to keep her hand from pulling him recklessly to her. But she couldn't keep her gaze from focusing on the sensuous curve of his lips.

"You still haven't told me why you shoved me off on your pushy salesman."

"Just a . . . business matter."

"No. I don't believe that. You've been afraid of something happening between us. Something like this."

His thigh was pressed against hers, her own unconsciously returning the pressure rather than retreating from it.

"We're . . . business acquaintances. Nothing more."

"I'd like to be more. A lot more."

She didn't respond, didn't dare, not with the tumult within her. His hand moved down to stroke the curve of her burlap-covered thigh. His eyes were narrowed in thought, and his touch more absentminded than seductive, but she felt the caress of each separate fingertip and longed to tear away the barrier of fabric and feel skin against skin.

Then anger overwhelmed Shar. Under the circumstances he had no right to suggest to her that he'd like to be something more than a business acquaintance! She stood up abruptly.

"We should figure out how we're going to sleep. We'll have to get up early. We may still have to hike out of here." She glanced around, deliberately ignoring the romantic dance of shadows from the flickering fire. "I'll take the sofa."

"And I suppose that means I'm supposed to gallantly retreat to the cold loft?"

She tightened the burlap sarong. "Suit yourself."

He did. He dragged the bare mattress down from the loft and spread it in front of the fireplace. There were no blankets. He took down the two remaining drapes, handed one to her and kept one for himself.

"Anyone going to worry when you don't come home tonight?" he asked.

"No one but Tripod. And she can go in and out her pet door. How about you?"

He shrugged, as if the matter was immaterial.

It was still much earlier than normal bedtime, but there seemed little else to do but to go to bed. The sudden tension between them precluded conversation. Tal removed his belt and shoes but kept his clothes on. Shar's clothes were almost dry but were stiff with dirt from the muddy puddle. She opted to sleep in the sarong and arranged the other burlap drape over her.

She lay with her back turned to the outside edge of the sofa, so that she wouldn't be looking down on Tal stretched out on the mattress before the fireplace. Within minutes she had reason to wish she'd chosen the soft old mattress. The sofa cushions were three bumps separated by rough ridges that bit into her ribs and legs.

She couldn't sleep, partially because it was too early, partially because of discomfort, partially because of her inner turbulence. Mostly, she knew, her wakefulness was a result of the intimacy of the situation, the simple disturbing fact of Tal's nearness.

Cautiously she shifted position on the sofa, turning so that her spine was pressed against the back of the sofa. Was Tal asleep? She couldn't tell. He was on his side, back turned to her, burlap drape pulled halfway over his head. If she moved just a few inches, she could reach out and touch him....

Resolutely she tucked her hands around her body, half afraid that in her sleep she might do exactly that. Perhaps it would be best if she did stay awake. Stay awake and figure out what was happening between them, what all this meant to Nicole, how or if she should tell Nicole any of it, how she was going to handle her own desires and emotions.

Yet once Shar had decided she should stay awake and think, sleep paradoxically became an irresistible force, dragging her eyes shut and clouding her mind. She drifted off, half woke once to see Tal in silhouette as he threw more wood on the fire, then drifted into sleep once more.

The next time she woke she was cold. She rose up on one elbow. The fire had died to glowing coals. Tal was now lying so that he faced her, the reddish glow of the embers reflecting on his skin, giving his innocent sleeping expression a faintly satanic cast. She snuggled deeper into the uncomfortable cushions and wrapped the drapes more tightly around her, but she was still cold, and unless someone put more wood on the fire it was going to go out completely.

Cautiously she threw the rough drape back, holding the loosened sarong around her body. She stepped over Tal and quietly pushed back the fireplace screen. She added more wood from the pile he'd stacked beside the hearth, then replaced the screen.

She started to step back across him, and something closed viselike around her ankle. His hand.

She looked down, saw the dark pools of his eyes staring up at her. It seemed almost as if the movement was a shock to him, too, as if he'd been motivated by primitive instinct beyond his control. She didn't move, didn't speak, yet messages arced between them.

Shar...

Tal...

And then she was sinking to the mattress beside him, the rough burlap falling open to expose the satin cream of her body. He buried his face between her breasts, husky wordless sounds coming from his throat.

Shar felt a moment of dismay, a twinge of conscience or fear, but both were feeble tappings on a distant door, too weak and remote to enter a space already filling with wild messages from her heart and senses. Pent-up longings overflowed, spilling out recklessly. This was wildest fantasy, deepest fear, sweetest dream and sensuous reality all tangled up in one. She wrapped her arms around him, kissing the dark hair on the top of his head as he moved from the lush valley between her breasts to the sensitive tips.

He circled the rosy halo around a nipple with his tongue, moving in smaller and smaller circles until he was at the very tip, and it rose, thrusting out to meet his caress, demanding more. He laughed in soft delight as he flicked the nipple with his tongue, sending dizzying, shivery tingles of delight shooting through her.

The wood she had placed on the fire suddenly caught, the fresh flames throwing a dancing light over their bodies. He lifted his head to look at her breasts, conveying that the sight was a sensual pleasure to be enjoyed along with touch.

"So lovely," he whispered. He turned to the other breast, the nipple already firm but not yet brought to the swollen peak of the first. He caressed it leisurely, filling his mouth with her and then drawing his lips to the very tip of the nipple. And at the same time his hand roamed her abdomen, fingertips playing gentle fire over her hipbone, the heel of his hand pressing deeper into her flesh with a more primitive rhythm.

"Tal...Tal...you're driving me crazy." She writhed gently beneath the hold of his lips, body arching toward him as coiled springs of desire wound tighter and tighter within her.

His mouth moved up to hers, lips so close that she felt their tantalizing brushing of hers when he whispered, "Crazy for what?"

Would he force her to say that she wanted him to make love to her? More than wanted it...needed it...ached for it? The thought angered her, and she challenged him with the tip of her own tongue, running it over his lips, penetrating the parted line just far enough to tempt him, not far enough to satisfy him.

"Tease," he growled, but he made the word more caress than complaint. His mouth came down on hers, the hard probe of tongue pushing hers into retreat, forcing her to submit to him. He slid over her, his clothed body pinning her naked form beneath him. She could feel the strength of his arousal, and he deliberately drove it against her. "You see? That's what happens to a tease."

"Really?" And she licked his lips again, adding a provocative nip on his lower lip.

He shifted his legs to surround her from the outside, then braced himself on one arm while he unbuttoned his shirt. He tossed it aside, then settled his bare chest against her breasts. He felt sleek and hard and warm against her skin. She ran her hands over his back, palms savoring the long muscles, fingertips caressing the ridge of his spine. Her fingers dipped beneath the waistband of the tan slacks and touched the bunched muscles below.

"And more things happen to a tease who does that," he warned. His hands slid down to tilt her hips to him, and he nudged her legs apart with a knee. He knelt between her knees and trailed kisses to her navel and below, then crossed the damp, scorching line with more kisses from hipbone to hipbone, finding a ticklish erotic spot she had never known was there.

She was beyond false modesty, beyond anything but wanting him, and she held him to her. "Now who's teasing whom?" she whispered.

He rolled away from her, and with a few swift movements removed the remainder of his clothes. He had a magnificent body. The firelight played over it like a dancing spotlight, highlighting the flat plane of his abdomen, sculpting his muscular thighs, glinting on the smooth skin. She followed the flickering light with her fingertips, blending sensual pleasures of sight and touch. And taking pleasure in knowing that he found just as great a pleasure in seeing and touching her.

And then there was no more teasing from either of them as he slid over her, movements swift and sure as he found the moist hollow of her femininity. For a few moments his strokes were hard and driving, almost savage, and she responded in kind, meeting him as fiercely as he came to her. She felt as if she was rocketing higher and higher, out of control—

His movements changed, slowing the rocket but prolonging the sweetness of the rise, widening the pleasure so that it wasn't a single streak but a broad band of sensuous delight. She could taste his mouth and skin, luxuriate in the possessive length of his body covering her, feel the racing tempo of his heartbeat. There was a delicious sense of timelessness to their lovemaking, as if forever were at her disposal, forever to feel him moving within her, to savor the sweet warmth of enveloping him.

And then to feel the sensations in her body undeniably converging on a single point, converging and tightening until the tension grew almost unbearable . . . and then releasing in wild waves of explosion. Her fingers bit into his shoulders, holding him as if only that kept her from being totally lost in the rainbow burst of ecstasy.

But even in that wild moment she was aware that only then did his moment of ultimate pleasure come, that he'd waited for her. Fleeting thoughts of a husband who had always taken his own satisfaction first, careless of hers, came back, and she was overwhelmed with wonder and with love for this generous man who now held her in his arms as if she was something fragile and precious. He rested his damp forehead against hers, making no move to separate himself from her, making her feel sweetly cherished.

"I think the fire is dying down again," she whispered eventually.

"Trying to get rid of me?"

She wrapped her legs around him fiercely. "No. Never!"

He laughed softly. "I'll throw on some wood and be right back."

He tossed wood on the fire, and she watched his silhouette against the blaze of fresh flames. He was not self-conscious in his nakedness, and she delighted in the ripple of his muscles and the sheen of his skin as he moved, even found a bold satisfaction in the appearance of his satisfied manhood. When he stepped back toward the mattress she clasped a hand around his ankle in imitation of what he had done to her.

He laughed and slid under the rough burlap covering with her. They lay with her head on his shoulder, legs entwined.

"Never again will I be deceived by that cool, professional businesswoman image of yours," he murmured. "Not when I know that underneath all that expensive tailoring is a woman who makes love like a passionate angel."

"Were you really deceived?"

"I had my suspicions from the very first."

"And here I thought you were just thinking about real estate all the time," she teased. She ran the sole of her foot up his leg, liking the feel of smooth relaxed muscle lightly roughened with masculine hair.

"I suppose it's a little late to ask, but you are protected, aren't you? The pill . . . ?"

Yes, it was a little late to ask, but she could hardly be angry or blame him for that; she had been as swept up in passion as he had. He had taken nothing that she hadn't eagerly given.

But no, she wasn't protected. For a moment she was angry. Did he think she did this sort of thing often, that she came prepared for it? Why wasn't he prepared? Yet at the same time she felt defensive about admitting that she wasn't prepared, that it had been a long, long time since she'd let a man get this close to her.

"I'm not exactly a twenty-eight-year-old virgin," she said with a certain coolness, as if that was answer enough to his question.

Absentmindedly Tal ran his fingers through her hair, lifting it and letting it fall, watching the firelight dance on the red and gold highlights. "Past marriage?"

She murmured a reluctant affirmative.

"Tell me about it?"

She hesitated, dismayed, wondering where to start. She'd tell him about her marriage to Matt; he'd tell her about Nicole. The past, the future, it would all come rushing in, tangling them in an impossible web. She couldn't face that tonight, not after what had just happened between them. Once they started talking everything would change. She could almost feel Nicole's hurt luminous eyes staring at her from beyond Tal's naked shoulder.

Tomorrow she would have to face those accusing eyes. Tomorrow she would have to consider the enormity of what had happened between them and what must be done about it.

But not tonight! This storm-bound cabin and this night were in a different dimension, unrelated to the world from which they had come and to which they must eventually return.

"No," she whispered back fiercely. "No talk about the past . . . or the future. . . . All there is, is *now*."

And in the now all that was important was the two of them and the passion that flared between them once more.

8

SUNLIGHT STREAMED through the uncurtained windows. Shar stretched luxuriously, feeling deliciously lazy and contented. Now she knew why cats purred, she thought dreamily. That's what she felt like doing.

"I thought you were going to sleep all day," Tal said. She had the not unwelcome feeling that he'd been standing there by the fire, watching her sleep. He bent down to give her a solid kiss on the mouth. He was already dressed and looked surprisingly neat except for his dark unshaven jaw. And even that could in no way be classified as *un*attractive.

"Maybe you should grow a beard," she suggested. She ran her fingertips over the bluish shadow, liking the rough masculine texture. "Makes you look a little wicked. And sexy."

"You're saying I need a beard to prove I'm sexy?"

She smiled reminiscently. "No, I don't think so."

She sat up and stretched again. The burlap fell to her waist, and she didn't bother to retrieve it. He leaned over again and planted a proprietary kiss on the tip of each breast, as if reminding her of an already staked claim.

"I'm afraid all I can find for breakfast is a couple of cans of sardines," he said.

She wrinkled her nose. "I think I'll pass."

"Planning to live on love?" he inquired.

She lay back against the mattress, still wearing only the glow that came from love and satisfied passion, her red-gold halo of hair fanned provocatively around her face. "Is that what you're offering as an alternative for breakfast?"

He grinned. "You may not have noticed, but we had *that* breakfast a little earlier."

"I noticed," she assured him. Oh, yes, she'd noticed. It was one of the reasons she felt like purring.

"And there's always lunch...." He smiled wickedly, then gave her another quick kiss. "But right now I'm going out to do something with the car. I put a pan of water on the fire to heat, if you want it."

The sunlight and crackling fire combined made the cabin comfortably warm this morning. Shar padded naked to the bathroom and washed up. Usually she took an abundance of hot water for granted, but this morning the single pan of it seemed the most glorious of luxuries. Afterward she shook as much dirt as she could out of her clothes and dressed.

"I'm working on the problem with the car," Tal called when she stepped outside. "There was some moisture condensed in the distributor cap. Not surprising, considering the storm and all the water we splashed through. I'm pulling the cap and drying it now. I think I'll dry the spark plug wires, too, and then we should be able to leave in a few minutes."

His words were enough to make Shar pause on the porch steps, and the image of Nicole's dark eyes suddenly rose up to condemn her. This was the tomorrow she had known must come, the day when she must step back into the real world and face the meaning and consequences of last night.

But not yet, she protested. Not yet! Not when Tal was smiling at her and the murmur of ocean waves was calling to her, not when the brilliant after-the-storm sunshine enveloped everything in glorious promise. Tal looked almost boyish, leaning into the car engine compartment, as carefree as a teenager with his first car. And Shar, she felt buoyant with love, light as a bubble dancing on the sea.

Wasn't it possible that somehow things could work out without anyone being hurt?

"No hurry," she called back. "I'm going down to the beach."

She paused at the sharp edge of the bluff, surprised at the width of beach below. Yesterday, storm and high tide had brought crashing waves into the jumbled driftwood, but now the water had withdrawn to expose a damp silver-gray band of sand littered with fresh driftwood and strands of olive-green kelp. Also now visible was a picturesque scattering of offshore rocks, and she spotted the sleek heads of several seals frolicking in the lift and fall of luminous green waves.

On impulse she slipped off her boots and rolled up her pantlegs. She skidded barefoot down the steep bank, the sand delightful between her toes.

She wandered along the beach, filling her jacket pockets with shells and rocks. She knew that once the rocks dried, their beauty would no doubt fade, but for now they were shimmering jewels. Tal joined her a few minutes later.

"The car is running fine now," he reported. "Ready to leave?"

"Are you?"

"Not really. But then I wasn't as fussy as you. I ate a can of sardines."

"I'll just live on love, thank you," Shar replied airily.

"Very well then, so that you don't run out of nourishment—" He put his arms around her and kissed her, holding her so tightly that he lifted her on her tiptoes. It wasn't a seductive kiss; it didn't say, "Let's go back and spend the day in bed." It was more an I'm-glad-to-be-with-you kiss, as cheerful as the grin that followed it.

Shar started to say the words that suddenly felt as natural as breathing. I love you. But she didn't, because love dragged in the future, and she wasn't ready to face that yet. Instead she said teasingly, "Now, that beats cold cereal any day."

"Isn't this something?" He looked out across the gently undulating surface of the sea. "Who'd have guessed it would be like this after last night?"

"Isn't there always a calm after a storm?"

"I hope so, because . . ."

Shar glanced up at him, surprised by an odd uneasy note in his voice.

"Because I'm afraid I may be walking straight into a storm right now. I wasn't going to tell you, but I guess I have to."

Shar suddenly felt a little dizzy. She wanted to run but couldn't. He was going to tell her about Nicole. No! Not yet, she protested silently. She knew it was something they had to face sooner or later, yet she desperately didn't want to face the complexity of the situation, her conscience and worries just yet. "Yesterday you accused me of sabotaging the car."

Shar blinked, a little taken back. "Did you?"

"There was moisture in the distributor cap. But I figured that out last night. I just didn't fix it. And then, just to make certain the car wouldn't start, I unfastened a couple of wires."

What he said was so far from what Shar had been expecting to hear that she could only look at him uncomprehendingly, as if he were spouting some foreign language. Finally she managed to ask, "Why?"

"Because I wanted to be with you. Talk to you. Arrange the situation so you couldn't back away from me as you always seem to do."

"We did a great deal more than talk!"

"I know. I didn't intend that.... At least not at first," he amended, smiling a little ruefully. "I just wanted to get closer to you. You're so damned elusive! I didn't figure on you taking off and falling in a puddle. Angry?"

"More like surprised, I suppose." Shar shook her head a little helplessly.

When she thought about it, though, she felt as if she'd just been given a reprieve, a few more moments of glorious freedom before she had to examine the past and future. There was just now, these still-wonderful moments to enjoy.

And she didn't want to waste a single one of them! She tossed away the weight that had begun to settle around her shoulders and slapped him on the arm. "Tag! You're it!" She sprinted away, challenging him to follow.

She raced down the beach, bare feet touching the packed sand so lightly that she felt almost airborne. But she'd gone no more than a dozen yards when he overtook her, his tag a bold slap on her derriere. Their laughter rang over the sound of the waves. The game reversed, and she was after him, thinking she hadn't a chance of overtaking him, until one of his shoes filled with sand and he had to stop. Then he took off both shoes and, barefoot, caught up with her, this time not content merely to tag her. He swept her up in his arms and waded ankle-deep into the foaming water.

She glanced over her shoulder at the cold froth. "You wouldn't!"

"What's in it for me if I don't?" he demanded. He hefted her up and down, as if considering how far he could toss her.

"What do you want?"

"Guess!" He leered and lifted her higher, taking an audacious lunge at her breast with his mouth.

"Did anyone ever tell you you're insatiable?" she grumbled.

"But I never was insatiable...until you came along." His mouth dipped to hers, and slowly he stood her upright, sliding her body the length of his as intimately and closely as the waves lapping the sand. She was vaguely conscious of the cold water sloshing around her ankles... but she'd have stood knee-deep in ice to capture the sweetness of that kiss. She wrapped her arms around his neck, wishing she could hold the moment forever.

He swallowed when he finally lifted his head. His eyes had a heavy-lidded, almost glazed look, the teasing gone. He touched her lips with a fingertip. "Shar..." He whispered her name with longing, but she knew instinctively that he wasn't just hungry for the passion they had already shared. He wanted something more. The dark cloud of the future loomed again—and again she refused to confront it.

"There's something about a man who eats sardines for breakfast that just drives me mad with desire," she whispered throatily.

For a moment he looked almost angry with her for dodging his seriousness, his tenderness, but then he laughed, and the moment passed. "I'll buy them by the carton," he assured her. "Maybe even the carload, if that's how you react."

They strolled back up the beach toward the cabin. The ribbon of sand stretched so far into the distance that even in sunshine it disappeared into a faint misty haze. They walked with arms companionably wound around each other's waists, dipping as if they were welded together to pick up a bit of shell or driftwood. Occasionally Shar kicked a foot through a ridge of beige-colored foam left by the sea and watched the bits of froth float away on the gentle breeze.

Kelp that had been broken off the seabed and flung ashore during the storm was everywhere. The rubbery bulbs tapered down to thick tubes and then to whiplike strands. Shar whimsically wrote her initials with two long strands, and Tal did likewise, breaking off a short piece to form the apostrophe between the *O* and *N* of his last name. He considered the results for a moment, then took two pieces of driftwood and crossed them between the two sets of initials.

"There, S.H. plus T.O'N."

Shar laughed. "I haven't seen anything like that—at least with my initials in it—since grade school. I didn't know you were such a romantic."

But she did, of course. She'd known it ever since that anniversary party, when he'd revealed his musings about a tenth wedding anniversary of his own.

"There are all kinds of things you don't know about me. And even more that I don't know about you." There was warm invitation in his voice, a hint that it was time they ventured beyond both the passion and the playfulness.

Shar refused to cooperate. "A woman is more desirable when she retains a bit of mystery, don't you think?" She deliberately tilted her head and batted her eyelashes with flirty exaggeration.

"I found you desirable when you were crawling around in the cobwebs looking for a trapped kitten. I found you desirable when you dumped me in a snowbank. I found you desirable when you were sitting wet and miserable in a mud puddle with tears streaming down your face. If I found you desirable all those times, I don't think losing some of the mystery is really going to affect anything." A thoughtful seriousness lurked beneath his teasing listing of events.

"I'm not mysterious, anyway," Shar protested. She tried for playfulness again. "After last night, what secrets could I possibly have left? You know every dimple, every mole—"

"That isn't what I meant, and you know it." Then his mouth curved in that wicked little grin she was beginning to know and love so well. "But I always did kind of wonder if redheads were red haired everywhere. And now I know."

"You mean I'm your first redhead?"

He looked down at her with an odd, thoughtful expression on his face. "You're my first . . . something," he said, as if he wasn't quite certain himself what it was.

They were just below the cabin then, looking up at their tracks angled across the steep sandy bank. They scrambled up to the grass and sat down to wipe sand from their feet and put on their shoes. Shar had the sobering feeling they were putting on something else along with their shoes, donning a maturity and responsibility she was loathe to assume, even though she knew those things couldn't be avoided. She felt as if they were relinquishing a magical time in another dimension.

They went inside the cabin and straightened up the room. Shar put the drapes back on their rods, and Tal dragged the mattress back to the loft. He took the wine bottle and empty chili can out to a trash barrel while she swept the accumulation of sand and dried mud out the door.

When they had finished, the cabin looked just as it had when they'd arrived. The burlap drapes appeared none the worse for wear after their night of unusual use. A faint smoky scent lingered in the air, but there was nothing to indicate that two people had shared a memorable night of passion here. Tal left a five-dollar bill on the counter—to pay for the food they had eaten, he said, in case the owner came and wondered where his chili and wine had gone.

"You haven't asked if I'm going to try to trade for the cabin," Tal said when they went outside.

Shar was ambivalent about knowing. "I guess we can talk about it when we get back to Portland."

He walked over to the car and put the hood down. Shar detoured to the edge of the bluff. Below, she could see their initials, still joined by the whimsical plus sign. But the incoming tide was already creeping toward the twisted strands of kelp, and soon they would be washed away.

She felt a tide inexorably creeping toward her, too. One she couldn't hold back much longer . . . and one she knew could wash away much more than a few initials on an idyllic beach.

Once away from the beach and the secluded cabin, Shar was uncomfortably conscious of the muddied look and gritty feel of her clothes. In Coos Bay she went into a big discount store and bought fresh clothing from the skin out. She changed in the ladies' room. Afterward they ate at the store's coffee shop. Breakfast hours were long over by then, so Shar settled for a salad lunch.

When Tal commented on her quietness she passed it off with an attempt at coquetry.

"That's what happens when a woman spends all night doing something . . . mmm . . . other than sleeping."

He grinned and leaned across the table to kiss her lightly. "You may just have to learn to get along with less sleep."

She smiled back, but it was a mechanical movement of lips. She felt that with each passing moment a crack between them was slowly widening, a crack that she knew Tal sensed in her withdrawal. Sensed but didn't understand.

The vague outline of Nicole's face, which Shar had blocked out of her mind, was inexorably drifting back, floating like an accusing wraith in the dim recesses of her thoughts. The magic of the night with Tal wasn't fading—it would never fade—but the blunt reality of the situation and all the feelings that she had avoided were crashing in on it.

Guilt. Disloyalty. She had made love with the man Nicole was in love with. She was in love with him herself. She had betrayed her best friend, and the knowledge hung like a yoke of stone on her shoulders.

And now what? Ignore last night, pretend it never happened? No, she couldn't do that! She was in love with Tal, even if she had no right to be. This wasn't some infatuation based on one night of magical passion. She'd known for days that she was falling in love with him, and last night had only made it soaringly obvious.

Suppose she didn't ignore it? Suppose she just closed her eyes to loyalty and responsibility and moral questions of right and wrong and ruthlessly snatched what she desperately wanted? Other women had done it. She could do it, too; she had no doubt that she could steal Tal away.

She also knew she would never do it. She wouldn't be able to live with herself if she did. Guilt and Nicole's hurt innocent eyes would haunt her forever.

Then *what*? Tell Nicole what had happened, beg her understanding? Nicole wouldn't fight or argue. She'd nod through tears and say she understood . . . and then she would disintegrate, just quietly wilt into nothingness. It had happened before, after Dave. This time would be even worse.

Shar loved Tal . . . and in an entirely different way, she loved Nicole. She was caught between them, torn like a flag claimed by opposing forces.

She wrestled with her thoughts all through the flight to Portland. She was conscious of Tal in the seat next to her, his shoulder occasionally brushing hers and his fingers entwining with hers. She nodded and smiled when he pointed out some particularly lovely view below, but she felt a kind of numbness that set her apart from the messages of her senses. With each passing mile she drew farther away from the magical island, closer to the harsh real world to which they were returning.

The plane landed on the clear sunny Portland runway just a few minutes past four o'clock. From the shelf above their seats Tal retrieved the sack that held her soiled clothes. They walked through the terminal building and out into late afternoon sunshine again. Shar felt as if much more than a single night had passed since she had left her car in the airport parking lot.

Tal fingered the darkening shadow of whiskers on his jaw. "I'll run home and get cleaned up, and then we'll get together for dinner later." He spoke as if their meeting later were a foregone conclusion. "Any place special you'd like to eat?"

"I'm really very tired."

"How about if I pick up something and bring it to your place?" He smiled engagingly, the flash of his teeth emphasized by the dark shadow of beard. "That is, if you think you know me well enough now to tell me where you live."

She looked up at him, realizing she'd been avoiding looking directly at him ever since they'd left the cabin. There was a concerned, puzzled expression on his face when she didn't immediately respond to his teasing comment, and her heart ached because of the two opposing forces tugging at her: love for him; loyalty to Nicole.

She swallowed. "Tal, it's been a...a wonderful trip, and we think we have ... certain feelings for each other. But maybe we should step back and take a ... a more objective look at the situation." Her tongue felt thick, unable to twist around the simple words. Because they weren't what she wanted to say. She wanted to throw her arms around him and shout, "I love you! I want to be with you tonight ... tomorrow ... forever."

"I wasn't suggesting that we move in together or make some lifetime commitment." He sounded a little stiff, perhaps even wary, but his smile softened the words, and he touched her cheek. "At least not for a day or two yet."

"Why don't I call you?"

He looked momentarily nonplussed; then the grin returned. "Okay, liberated lady. You work out whatever it is that's bothering you and then call me. But don't make me wait too long. I'm not the patient type."

Shar went to her car after turning down Tal's offer to see her home. He pulled out of the parking lot ahead of her, giving her a little backward wave.

She just sat there in her car, clutching the steering wheel, wishing she had some justification for her actions. Love. Wasn't love supposed to conquer all? She was in love with Tal. But was that enough to justify the way she had betrayed Nicole's trust in her? And what about the way Tal had betrayed Nicole? The faithful man, tested and proven...except that he wasn't really so faithful, after all.

That thought only slowly crept into Shar's consciousness, only gradually penetrated her burden of guilt. A peculiar disorienting dizziness took hold; her perspective shifted to a different corner of the triangle. She had been wrapped up in worry about how or whether to tell Nicole about what happened, apprehensive of Nicole's reaction. She had been weighed down by her conscience, tangled in thoughts of how she and Tal might somehow work things out without hurting Nicole.

Amid all those agonizing worries and concerns, though, there was one small point she had neglected to consider. She had fallen in love with a man who had just proven he couldn't be faithful.

No, he hadn't been unfaithful *to* her; he had been unfaithful *with* her. Perhaps that was why it had taken her until this bitter moment to recognize the truth of his character. This wasn't the viewpoint from which she had usually observed the unfaithful man. And yet that was what Tal was. Unfaithful.

Grimly she reflected on all those times she had given him the benefit of the doubt or rationalized his questionable actions, all those times she'd decided she was misinterpreting some word or deed and judging him unjustly. She had misinterpreted nothing! Her first suspicions had been all too correct. He was just like all the others, like her father, like Matt, like Dave Dusek, too. Even if by some miracle things worked out so that Nicole wouldn't be hurt, so that Shar and Tal could be together with Nicole's blessing, what would Shar have? An unfaithful man. If he could be unfaithful with her, he could be unfaithful to her. If he could leave another woman for her, he could leave her for another woman. And no amount of magnetic charm or sexiness could compensate for that fatal flaw.

The bitter disappointment and disillusionment crashed over her like the storm-lashed waves of the day before.

She didn't want a man like that. No, never, never again! No matter if he was handsome and exciting and teasing and romantic, no matter that he carried her to soaring heights of physical ecstasy, no matter that even as she damned him she loved him...somehow, some way, some time she would get over him.

Let some other woman have him, Shar thought wildly. Let him enchant some other woman . . . and then tear her apart with his infidelity. He wasn't going to do it to her!

And then her thoughts tumbled chaotically in another direction. Nicole was that other woman! He had already enchanted her, already made her fall in love with him, and someday he might destroy her as Dave almost had. She had to tell Nicole, warn her. Frantically she started the engine.

Just as quickly, her frenzy to reach Nicole vanished. She had come full circle, back to the point of her first worries. She couldn't tell Nicole because it was already too late, because Nicole was already in love with Tal, and the knowledge of his betrayal would destroy her. The time for testing, when Nicole might have been able to bear disappointment, was long past.

Shar drove toward home feeling dazed. She had fallen into a trap; no matter which way she turned she ran into an insurmountable, impenetrable wall. She stopped for gas and felt only a kind of weary resignation when the attendant pointed out that she had a tire going flat. She told him to fix it and then just sat with hands folded in her lap while the work was done.

She didn't reach her apartment until almost six-thirty. Tripod was gratifyingly happy to see her, even though the kitten hadn't gone hungry. There was still dry cat food in her dish. Shar picked up the kitten and hugged her, grateful for the uncomplicated love that it was possible to share with this little creature.

She was in the shower washing her hair, when the phone rang. She didn't mind being unable to answer the call. She suspected it was Tal, and even though angry scathing dialogues with him kept running through her mind, she was in no mood to talk to him.

The phone rang again when she was blow-drying her hair. Shar was half-inclined just to let it ring, but Tripod pounced on the instrument, as usual, and knocked off the receiver. Shar braced herself to resist the tempting magic of Tal's voice and picked up the phone.

"Shar, Shar, where have you been? I've been calling and calling!"

"I had a flat tire on the way back from the airport—" Shar broke off, realizing Nicole didn't really want to know where she'd been. Nicole was simply frantic because Shar hadn't been there when she'd needed her. Her friend's voice was wild and panicky, hoarse with sobs.

"Nikkie, what's the matter?" Shar asked sharply. "What's happened?"

Even before Nicole answered the question in broken words, Shar knew what must have happened. Tal. He had callously gone straight to Nicole's house from the airport and broken off with her, with never a thought for her sensitive feelings. Nicole was just someone he wanted to get rid of now, and he had discarded her with all the ruthlessness the rumors said he was capable of. Shar felt no joy, although he had evidently done it for her. This action did nothing to make his unfaithfulness of last night any less dishonorable. All this said was that when a new desirable woman came along he was perfectly willing to discard the old one without a backward glance.

"Nikkie, get hold of yourself. I'm coming right over. Just go sit on the sofa and don't move, and I'll be right there." Shar put all her authority into the instructions, only hoping Nicole would comply. She remembered all too well the way Nicole had wandered around in a daze that other time. She'd actually fallen on the concrete floor in the garage and cracked a bone in her ankle. "Where's Cindy?"

"This is spring vacation at school. She went down to stay with my parents in Palm Springs for the week."

"Good." Palm Springs was where Nicole should go for a few days, Shar decided. If necessary, she'd fly down there with Nicole to make certain she got there safely. And then Shar was going to give Tal an explosive piece of her mind.

Shar didn't bother to finish styling her hair. She ran a comb through the damp strands and pinned them back with two barrettes, noting that the effect was incongruously ingenue, considering the circumstances. A scarlet letter on her forehead would be more appropriate. She threw on jeans and a sweatshirt, gave Tripod an apologetic caress for leaving again so soon and dashed down to her car.

Shar didn't bother with the doorbell at Nicole's. She let herself in with the key she'd had ever since she'd practically lived at the house following the breakup of Nicole's marriage. She found Nicole obediently sitting on the living room sofa, legs tucked under her. Her face was puffy and blotchy from crying, her cheeks tear streaked, her dark hair limp and untidy from the many times she had run her fingers through the short curls.

All this so soon, Shar thought in dismay. It couldn't have been more than a couple of hours since Tal had been here, and Nicole looked as if she'd been in a state for days. Damn Tal! How could he have done this to her?

But then she had to damn herself, as well, because she was as much to blame as Tal. The only good thing about the situation was that now they both knew Tal for what he was. Now his true character was out in the open, and it was up to Shar to keep this from destroying Nicole. She roughly pushed her own pain and despair into the background; she'd have to confront her heartbreak over Tal eventually, but for now it would have to wait.

Shar went to her friend and put strong comforting arms around her. Nicole started crying again; Shar simply held and rocked her, murmuring words of solace, knowing the soothing sounds were more important than the words themselves.

"I'm sorry," Nicole gasped finally. She rubbed her eyes with an already shredded tissue. "Every time something happens I drag you in and dump all my troubles on you."

"That's what friends are for. Have you called your therapist yet, the woman you saw before?"

"Therapist?" Nicole repeated vaguely. "I think she moved away."

So there was no immediate help available from that direction. "Have you had anything to eat?"

Nicole considered the question with wrinkled brow, as if she were under cross-examination and it was important to be very precise in her answer. "Since when?"

"It doesn't matter. I'll fix something."

"I'm not hungry."

"Tea, then. You stay right here."

Shar prepared tea in the kitchen and returned a few minutes later with two steaming cups. Nicole hadn't moved. She wasn't crying, but Shar knew that wasn't necessarily a sign of improvement. Nicole appeared almost numb, as if trying to shut out the pain.

Shar set the cups of tea on the coffee table to cool, afraid Nicole might burn herself on the hot liquid and not be aware of it.

"Can you tell me what happened?" Shar asked.

"Tal came by. He said we were through."

"Just like that?"

A bit of scornful animation came to Nicole's face, a sudden flush of color beneath the tear stains. Good, Shar thought. Anger was better than blank withdrawal.

"Oh, no. You know Tal."

Shar closed her eyes momentarily. Yes, she knew Tal. Knew his mouth and body, knew his kisses and caresses. Knew he could take her to the peaks of ecstasy...and drop her to the pits of despair. She forced herself to say, "What did he do?"

"I wasn't expecting him. He just showed up. He acted kind of uncomfortable and awkward. Then he started telling me how much respect he had for me and how highly he thought of me and what a good mother I was to Cindy. You'd have thought he was about to give me a Housewife of the Year award. But what I thought—oh, stupid, blind, naive me—I thought he was getting ready to propose. And then he dumped it on me, how I'd make some man a wonderful wife someday, and he wished me every happiness. And we wouldn't be seeing each other anymore."

"Did he say why he was doing it?"

Nicole shrugged. She reached for the tea and took a sip. "He didn't have to. He's met someone else. It was written all over him. The fingerprints practically glowed. In fact he's probably been seeing her on the sly all along." Nicole suddenly stood up and stared at her reflection in the ornately framed mirror over the sofa, perhaps searching for the flaws in herself that had caused him to turn away.

"Oh, Nikkie, I doubt that he was seeing someone...." Tal hadn't actually been "seeing" her, at least not in the sneaking-around sense Nicole was implying. They'd just been thrown together by business matters.

So was she defending him? No way!

Nicole's momentary animation drained away; she was like a mechanical doll gone dead. She slumped back onto the sofa and clasped a throw pillow to her stomach.

"Shar, what's going to happen to me?" Her voice was small and bewildered. "It's all happening again just like the first time. And I was so sure Tal was different, that he was strong and dependable."

"I know." Shar helplessly patted Nicole's cold arm.

"I had this beautiful radiant dream. I saw us as a happy family. Cindy with a wonderful caring father, me with a loving devoted husband, one who would never, ever stray. And I'd be the perfect wife, with dinner ready every night and the house clean and inviting, and we'd have friends and go places and do things together." She stroked the fringe on the throw pillow, one she'd made herself. "And it was all just a foolish fantasy, like the time my parents gave me a beautiful perfect little dollhouse for Christmas, and I played a game, imagining myself becoming very tiny and living in it."

And at about that time in her own life, Shar thought wryly, she had encountered her father passionately kissing a strange woman in the kitchen while her mother was in the living room with the other guests at a Christmas party. Neither childhood experience, different as they had been, had prepared Nicole or Shar for coping with the pain of loving an unfaithful man when they were adults.

"What's going to become of me, Shar?" Nicole repeated. She reached for Shar's hand, as if for an anchor. "It's all just the same as before. I—I can feel the pieces of *me* coming apart."

"No. No, it isn't the same as before. And you're not going to come apart. You're not the same woman you were the other time. You're a survivor, Nikkie! You made it through the other time, and you'll make it through this time."

"I don't think so. . . ."

"But it's true. You're stronger than you think. Stronger than *I* thought you were." Shar's voice was low and fierce, and she was suddenly convinced of what she was saying. Nicole *had* come a long way. "Look at yourself. You can sit here and make a little joke about Tal giving you a Housewife of the Year award—"

"Some joke!"

"Well, it's probably not going to make it into some big-time comedian's routine," Shar conceded, "but it's something you couldn't have done the other time. And telling me that Tal looked as if he had fingerprints all over him. . ."

Shar paused for a moment, trapped in bittersweet guilty memory. Those were *her* fingerprints. Then she rushed on.

"Maybe your dream was a . . . a little unreal. A little too perfect. But that doesn't mean you can't find a good life, a wonderful life. There are lots of other dreams. Go after what you want. Do what's best for you, not what anyone else thinks is best. Life doesn't have to revolve around a man."

"I think for me . . . maybe it does."

"Then someday you'll find him! Just don't let this man's flaws make you believe there are some terrible flaws in *you*. You're a wonderful woman and mother, Nikkie, a beautiful person both inside and out. You're sweet and generous, and I couldn't love you any more if you were my real sister. This man should . . . should kick himself in his own behind for being stupid enough to let you go."

Nicole suddenly giggled, even though tears shimmered in her eyes. "I think that is anatomically impossible."

"Anyone who can say *anatomically* without getting her tongue twisted can't be in too bad a shape." She put an arm around Nicole's shoulders and shook her lightly. "Now let's fix something to eat, okay?"

Nicole went to wash her face, and Shar went to the kitchen. She deliberately fumbled the dinner preparations, and Nicole took over. Shar knew that was good for Nicole in two ways. It kept her hands and mind busy, and it helped her restore a more positive image of her abilities. The quick dinner Nicole prepared was delicious, and Shar told her so.

"I love to cook," Nicole agreed. "You know, I was majoring in home ec at college before I dropped out to marry Dave, and I used to think that maybe I'd start a small catering service someday."

"That's a marvelous idea, Nikkie. You see? There are all sorts of marvelous opportunities just waiting for you to reach out for them."

"But I'd rather be married to a man I love."

"No reason you can't do both."

They talked long into the night, and Nicole kept coming up with more ideas. Shar was pleased at first, but then she realized that Nicole was soaring too high, that she had swung from lethargic hopelessness to hyperactive exhilaration. Shar knew it was quite possible that her friend was going to need professional help, but that night Shar managed to talk her down to a calmer level and tucked her into bed.

The following morning Nicole appeared to be on a more normal, less fluctuating plane. She ruefully shrugged off some of last night's wilder ideas as "rejection mania." She seemed introspective and thoughtful, less communicative than usual. She washed her hair and looked more like her usual self. Shar suggested that she go down to Palm Springs to be with her parents and Cindy, and Nicole said she'd think about it.

Shar stayed with Nicole all morning, but by noon Shar felt confident enough to leave her while she went to the office. In fact, Nicole urged her to go, saying she'd be fine. Shar promised to return right after work.

At the office Lil greeted Shar with wails of "Where have you *been*?" There had been a million phone calls, Lil said. Tons of mail.

Shar smiled at the exaggerations. "I knew this office couldn't operate without me." She didn't explain her absence. "By the way, did Mr. O'Neal call? Talcott O'Neal?"

"No, I don't think so."

So he was being temporarily patient. "If he does call, I don't want to talk to him. Not under any circumstances. I don't care what you tell him, just don't put him through."

Shar stayed at the office until a little after five-thirty, slogging her way through phone calls and paperwork. She swung by her apartment to make sure Tripod had food and water, then returned to Nicole's house.

She rang the doorbell, but there was no answer, so she dug the key out of her purse. She found the note on the kitchen counter.

Shar,
Thanks for everything, for being the most loyal friend, the best almost sister in the world. I know you won't approve of what I'm planning to do, but it's

what I have to do. It's what is best for me.

Love forever 'n ever,
Nikkie

Shar stared at the note, turned it over as if the other side might hold the key to the enigmatic words. Where had Nicole gone? What was she going to do?

She could have decided to go to Palm Springs . . . or maybe she just needed to be alone to think. But those weren't actions of which Shar would disapprove, and the note had such a terrible, determined ring of finality.

Shar was still staring at the note when the doorbell rang. She dashed to the door. Perhaps Nicole was back already. She was always forgetting her key, laughing at herself for being so scatterbrained. Shar flung the door open.

And looked directly into the astonished eyes of the man who had so recently whispered that she made love like a passionate angel.

9

"WHAT ARE YOU DOING HERE?" Tal asked. He took a step backward. His expression was both surprised and puzzled, the look of a man who has stumbled into the wrong house.

"Nicole is my friend." Shar stood in the doorway as though prepared to physically block his entrance. "What are *you* doing here?"

He ignored the question. "What the hell do you mean, Nicole is your friend? She never mentioned you. And you never mentioned her. What's going on? Where is she?"

Shar thrust the note at him. The handwriting was rounded and graceful, even though the note had obviously been written in haste. Nicole had had this plan, whatever it was, in mind even before Shar had left for the office, Shar realized. Looking back, she recognized that Nicole had been anxious to get her out of the house. In order to do what?

"Nicole would never deliberately do herself physical harm," Tal said.

"No? Then why is doing herself harm the first thought that comes to your mind?" That thought had also flashed instantly into Shar's mind.

"Did she go in her car? Take a suitcase?"

"I don't know. I just got here."

Tal brushed by her, sweeping her out of the way with a rough stroke of his arm. He looked in the garage first; Nicole's Lincoln was gone. Shar's immediate relief that Nicole wasn't lying in a carbon-monoxide-filled car was followed by the worry that her friend was surely in no condition to be driving anywhere. Why, *why* hadn't she stayed with Nicole? Why did she keep letting her best friend down?

Tal strode from the garage to the bedroom wing of the big house.

He tore through the closets in Nicole's bedroom. He found two designer suitcases. He shoved the mirrored sliding door shut so savagely that Shar expected the glass to shatter. "Well, you're her friend, so you claim. What do you think? Is there a suitcase missing or not?"

"I don't know. She and Dave used to do some traveling."

He gave her a narrowed glance, and she realized her statement revealed that her relationship with Nicole was one of long standing. His hard expression as he considered that information was enough to make a shiver of apprehension run up her back. She could also see him grimly weighing priorities, filing the information away as something to check on later, after Nicole was taken care of.

"Was she upset before she wrote the note?" he asked.

"Of course she was upset!" Shar retorted. "After what you did to her—"

He turned from where he had been pawing through the items on Nicole's dressing table. "And just what, exactly, are you accusing me of doing to her?"

"You know what you did to her! You led her on, made her believe you were going to marry her and then dumped her as if she were yesterday's newspaper!"

"I don't know exactly where you got your information about my relationship with Nicole—"

"Where do you suppose I got it? From her! She was in love with you. She could never stop talking about you—"

"We'll discuss that later." Again that harshly efficient ordering of priorities. "How did you get in here? Did she leave the house unlocked?"

"No. I have a key." Another revealing bit of information for him to stash away. A time of reckoning was coming, she knew, and it wasn't far off. "I stayed here last night. She was in very bad shape, but she seemed much better this morning. I wouldn't have left her alone if I hadn't thought she was okay. But apparently I was wrong."

"Not necessarily. Perhaps she decided to go see her parents in Palm Springs. Cindy is there for the week."

They briefly discussed the pros and cons of calling Nicole's parents. Nicole couldn't be there yet, even if that was where she was heading, but she might have called to tell them she was coming. Though that hardly correlated with her disturbing comment about Shar's disapproval of what she was doing. They didn't want to upset Nicole's parents and Cindy prematurely, of course. They finally decided that Shar should call Cindy and fish around to see if she could learn anything.

The maid who answered the phone said that both Cindy and her grandparents were out. Shar, without leaving her name, said she'd call back later.

Her hand remained on the receiver when she put the phone down. They were sitting in the formal living room, which was done in delicate shades of blue and cream and orchid. Tal's eyes had a hard glitter, more steel than gold, and the contrast between the pastel surroundings and his rugged frame and dark hair intensified her sense of lurking danger.

"I think," he said, "it's time for explanations." He spoke slowly and very distinctly, as if to make certain she understood this was not merely a casual request.

She tried an accusing bluff. "And I think it's time you explained what you're doing here. Don't you think you've hurt Nikkie enough already?"

"I was . . . worried about her." Sounding a little grudging, as if he didn't want to admit to any part of Shar's bitter accusations, he added, "She did take my telling her that I wouldn't be seeing her again somewhat harder than I expected."

"She was stunned," Shar said flatly. "Wiped out."

"You obviously knew I was seeing Nicole. Did she also know about you and me?"

"She knew all there was to know, that we were acquainted on a professional basis."

He laughed humorlessly. "Is that what you call our night at the cabin?" When Shar didn't reply he added, "Let's get back to your friendship with Nicole."

"Nikkie and I have been friends since junior-high days. I spent a lot of time at her house when . . . when things were going badly at my own. We roomed together at college. She was there for me when my marriage broke up, and I tried to do the same for her when her husband left her for another woman. We didn't really share the same social or business lives, but we were best friends. *Always* best friends," she added almost fiercely, as if to deny whatever he might be thinking about her actions.

"So why all this secrecy? Why was I the only one who didn't know we were involved in this little triangle?"

"There was no triangle! Nikkie is in love with you. She thought you were in love with her. And then you were unfaithful to her." Shar stumbled over the words as bitter guilt about her own involvement battered her again.

"I'd say that you're using a rather rigid definition of unfaithfulness. I—"

"She thought you were going to ask her to marry you. She trusted you, and you betrayed her! You were unfaithful—"

"Unless you told her about our night at the cabin, she didn't even know about it. I haven't told her."

"And is that your standard, the typical arrogant male standard, that so long as a woman doesn't know about unfaithfulness, that makes it quite all right?" Shar asked in a voice laced with scorn. "And it's also okay to dump one woman for another whenever you feel like it, no matter how you hurt that woman? You're worse than I thought, no better than any of the others!"

"I don't feel that I gave Nicole reason to believe I was committed to her. If she read more into our relationship than was actually there—"

"You were tested and proven! She had every reason to believe you would be utterly faithful to her, that you were a man who could be trusted and relied upon. Even *I* believed it!" Shar's fingertips flew to her lips to shut off the accusing, incriminating words, but it was too late. And Tal's sharp mind zeroed in immediately.

"What do you mean, 'tested and proven'?"

"Nothing." Shar kept her gaze on the pale blue carpet, avoiding his eyes. "Just a . . . figure of speech."

"Like hell it is." She could feel him studying her, and she shivered lightly under the cold appraisal. "I have the distinct impression that this has something to do with that little veil of mystery you've always hidden behind."

"I keep my personal life separate from my dealings with clients!"

"Really?" His faint smile challenged her statement, and she felt her chill turn to a hot flood of humiliation at what the single word insinuated . . . not without justification, considering that night at the cabin on the coast. But he apparently decided not to pursue that line of inquiry, at least for the moment. "What convinced *you* that I was this paragon of virtue, incapable of looking at another woman besides Nicole? I will get it out of you, Shar," he added softly when he saw the stubborn set of her jaw, "if we have to stay here all night before you tell me."

There was an implied threat behind the words. Physical threat? No. In spite of the capacity for ruthlessness that she'd seen in him when his property had been vandalized, she doubted he'd use force against a woman. But he was quite capable of physically holding her prisoner here until she told him what he wanted to know.

Reluctantly she asked, "Do you remember an anniversary party given a while back by some people named Calvert? You and Nikkie were supposed to go, and then she told you at the last minute that she couldn't make it."

He nodded warily.

"You met a woman there. A blonde wearing a skimpy harem-girl costume. She . . . came on very strong to you. Even invited you into her apartment after the party. You turned her down cold."

"She was a friend of yours? She told you what happened?"

"The harem girl was . . . me. In a veil and a blond wig."

"You!" He leaned forward to look at her, his piercing gaze searching her incredulously for some sign of similarity to that other woman.

"It was a little scheme Nikkie and I cooked up to test you, to see if you could be tempted into being unfaithful. And when you couldn't be, we both thought you were totally dependable, that you weren't going to be lured away by some scheming little sexpot, the way Nicole's husband was."

He leaned back. "I see. And I assume this was your clever idea?"

"I don't believe whose idea it was really matters," Shar said defensively, determined not to give away any more than she already had.

"I suppose not. In any case, apparently Nicole wasn't exactly the sweet uncomplicated creature I always thought she was. I must admit that it was a rather inventive, if not necessarily an ethical, scheme." His tone was more dry than angry, but it hardened as he added, "You were, by the way, very good at playing the part. Very provocative and tempting."

"But you *weren't* tempted. You weren't even interested. And so we both believed—"

"What if I had been interested? What if I had jumped at your invitation to come up to your apartment and get 'better acquainted'? What would you have done then?"

Shar evaded that issue. "That doesn't matter now. I realize that what Nikkie and I did was perhaps a bit…underhanded, but it was something we both felt had to be done. Tal, Nikkie was devastated when Dave abandoned her in favor of a woman he'd apparently been sneaking around with for some time! She came very close to having a complete breakdown. We both knew she couldn't risk having it happen again. And now it has."

"I'm very sorry about what happened to Nicole in the past. She never gave me any details of the breakup of her first marriage. I didn't know anything about it. I can see that it must have been very rough on her. I'm also sorry if my actions have hurt her. But the fact remains that she apparently read a great deal more into our relationship than was actually there." In spite of the apology, there was an unyielding quality to Tal's voice. It was a potent reminder of that hard ruthless facet Shar had occasionally glimpsed. His tenderness and concern went only so far; inside was the steel core that had kept him going when his father had died, that now made it possible for him to take an unemotional view of Nicole's problems. "I never made any commitments to her. I never told her I loved her. I never asked her to marry me."

"Tal, Nikkie may be somewhat naive for a woman her age, but she most certainly isn't stupid! If she thought you were planning to ask her to marry you, she undoubtedly had some concrete reason to believe it. Are you trying to tell me you never even considered marrying her?"

He frowned. "I considered it—" He stood up abruptly, a muscle working at the angle of his jaw. "I need a cup of coffee."

He strode directly to the coffee maker in the kitchen, hands plucking the coffee canister and cups out of the cabinet with familiarity. Shar stood in the arched doorway between kitchen and dining room. It hadn't been so very long ago that she had first heard Tal's name right here. He turned to face her when he had the coffee started, his arms folded across his chest, his expression moody.

Shar waited several long moments for him to speak, and when he didn't, she prodded him with the incriminating facts. "You've been seeing Nikkie for weeks now. She said Cindy was crazy about you, that you gave her skiing lessons. She said you took them to the coast and to Mount Hood, that you liked her cooking. And that you were making sounds like a man who was ready to get married and settle down, even if you hadn't actually proposed yet."

He still didn't say anything. The coffee maker gave a final sigh and shut off. Tal filled the cups. Shar stepped forward to pick one up, then retreated to the arched doorway again.

"I told you about how the business my father and I were in together almost went bankrupt and how he was killed and how I'd worked for years to get the company to where it is now."

His voice was heavy, as if he spoke under a burden of guilt. Shar knew the feeling, but she resolutely refused to acknowledge her sympathy for him.

"I had some . . . relationships with women during those years, but the business was all that really mattered to me. My personal life was strictly secondary. Then a while back I finally came to a pause point in my life. I looked around and saw that the business was a going, growing concern. There are still a lot of problems, of course, as there are in any business, but it's a success. I'd reached that goal. But my personal life was damned empty. Then I met Nicole. Perhaps she told you how we met."

"Yes."

Tal stood with his back to the counter, the palm of one hand lightly cupping the elbow of his other arm as he held the coffee cup. "I looked...and I liked what I saw. A good woman. Attractive, warm, easy to be with. And I liked Cindy, too. We got along great. I knew I could raise her as if she were my own. Together, Nicole and Cindy were a nice neat package of domestic tranquility, all the things I suddenly realized I'd been missing all these years."

"Then why—"

"There was just one small drawback to the whole deal. I wasn't in love with Nicole. Lord knows I tried to fall in love with her. I *wanted* to fall in love with her. Nicole seemed to be everything a man could ever want in a wife. But it just didn't happen. And then you came along."

Shar closed her eyes and leaned a little dizzily against the archway. Those were the words she hadn't wanted to hear, the words she had dreaded. "I never tried—"

"I know you didn't. I can see that now. But—"

"Would you have broken up with Nikkie if you and I hadn't met?"

"I don't know. But the fact is we did meet, and that changes everything." He took the coffee cup from her stiff hands and placed it on the tile counter. His hands closed around her upper arms, his touch gentle but with a warning strength in it. Before he could go on, the sound of the kitchen telephone made them jump, their sharp reactions out of proportion to the soft unthreatening brrr.

They both said, "I'll get it." Then Tal backed off and nodded at Shar to take the call. "If it's Nicole, she'd probably rather talk to you."

It wasn't Nicole. It was a woman calling to remind Nicole of the luncheon meeting of some charity committee Nicole was on. Shar said she'd relay the message. She had a sinking feeling when she hung up the receiver. Where *was* Nicole?

"Do you think we should call the police?" Shar asked.

"I don't think they'll act unless someone has been missing longer than Nicole has been gone."

"But the note—"

"Let's wait until we get hold of her parents or Cindy. We may be overdramatizing."

Shar tried again to reach Nicole's parents' number in Palm Springs. Same maid, same answer.

This time Tal turned her into his arms when she hung up the receiver on the wall-mounted telephone. Shar longed to accept the comfort of his embrace, to rest her head against his shoulder and abandon herself to his strength and security. But she didn't. She remained stiff, hands pressed against his chest to keep their bodies apart, eyes focused just below his mouth. Guilt, that emotion with which she was becoming all too painfully familiar, assaulted her again, little knives of accusation and remorse cutting deeper and deeper into her conscience.

But it wasn't guilt alone that kept her rigid and unyielding in the circle of Tal's arms. Some small part of her thoughts and emotions stayed separate in a small room off by themselves, and they were targeted solely, with crystal clarity, on what *Tal* had done.

"Sweetheart, I'm sorry about Nicole. I never wanted to hurt her, any more than you did. I'm as worried about her as you are. But we have you and me to consider, too, and we can't let this tear us apart."

Shar tilted her head to look up at him, her eyes a chill green sea of anger. "How can you even think of you and me at a time like this, when Nikkie may be—"

"At the moment we can't do anything for Nicole but wait."

"And so how do you suggest that we pass the time away? Go in and make love on her bed? Maybe she'll come home and find us. That should make the situation brilliantly clear to her, just in case we've failed to destroy her completely!" She pounded his chest with her closed fists, taking out on him the fury of her frustration.

"Shar, stop it!" He grabbed her wrists and forced them around behind her back. He pressed her against the wall, his hard body holding her imprisoned so that she could do no more than writhe helplessly. "What's happened between us has happened, and there's no point in denying our feelings for each other."

"What feelings?" Shar taunted. "Passion? Lust?" With her body crushed between his rugged male form and the wall, she could feel the faint stirrings of arousal within her.

And they increased even as she hated herself for having them, her breasts meeting the pressure of his chest even as she tried to retreat against the wall, internal organs softening with desire even as outer muscles tensed in anger and resistance.

"I'm talking about love." But she could feel passion stirring in his body, too. She wouldn't give in to it again, she vowed fiercely, not now, not ever!

"I could never love a man who can't be faithful!"

His mouth had been moving toward hers, but her words jolted him to a halt. "What the hell is that supposed to mean?" he demanded.

"I think the words explain themselves."

"You mean you're telling me that you consider me to be some sort of cheater because I made love with *you*?" He sounded incredulous, and he moved his upper body away just enough so that he could get a better look at her face. "I can't believe—"

"Faithfulness is like pregnancy. You are or you aren't. There's no halfway point. You were unfaithful to Nicole. The fact that it was with me is . . . irrelevant."

"By any normal set of standards I wasn't unfaithful!"

"Whose standards? Yours? If a man can be unfaithful with me, he could be unfaithful to me!"

"Well, aren't you the high-and-mighty, holier-than-thou one!" His mouth twisted in scorn, and he released her, letting go so abruptly that she staggered. If she hadn't caught herself against the counter she would have fallen, but he made no move to aid her. He started to turn away from her in disgust, but instead, he looked back at her, his gaze narrowing. "Somehow I doubt that my actions alone, reprehensible as you seem to believe they are, were enough to give you this inflexible, carved-in-granite standard of

what establishes the line between faithfulness and unfaithfulness."

"What you did just proved to me that you're like all the
others. Like Nikkie's husband, Dave. Like my father. He
had a *most* flexible attitude about what constituted faithfulness. As long as my mother didn't know what he was
doing behind her back, it didn't count. And if she did find
out, he'd beg and plead and promise never to do it again,
and she'd cry and take him back. I can't begin to count the
number of times all that happened. And during those
times I'd take refuge at Nikkie's house with Nikkie's family, where everything was always peaceful and calm and
stable."

"Are your parents still doing this, or did they eventually break up for good?"

"My father was killed in a car wreck in California. I received a phone call at college telling me that both my parents had been killed." She smiled with a bitter lack of
humor. "As it turned out, the woman with whom he was
traveling...and registering with at motels as husband and
wife...was not my mother." Shar paused, swallowed and
tried to calm the conflicting emotions that always assaulted her when she thought about her father. She had
loved him even though she had hated the things he'd done
and the pain he'd caused; she supposed he'd loved her too,
in his way. But he'd usually had too many nonpaternal relationships going to maintain any real father-daughter relationship. "My mother has remarried. She lives in San
Francisco now."

"She married a different type of man? One who can be
faithful?"

Shar nodded. Clyde Perkins was neither as handsome
nor as charismatic as Shar's father had been. Some people probably even thought him a little dull and unsophis-

ticated. But he had Shar's total respect and admiration and approval. He was faithful. "I think she's happy now."

"Then you'll have to admit that there *are* some faithful men around. Your mother found one." When Shar didn't comment he picked up his cup of coffee and took a sip. Shar knew the coffee must be cold by now, but he didn't seem to notice. "But apparently you didn't."

"No."

"Why wouldn't you tell me about your marriage when we were at the cabin?"

"Because I didn't want to think about the past or the future." Brutally she confronted what she had refused to face then. "Because I knew what we were doing was wrong, yet I didn't have the strength or courage not to do it."

He chose to neither confirm nor deny her self-recriminations. "Tell me about your marriage."

"I don't see that it matters—"

"*Tell me.*"

Shar turned away from him. "I met Matt Provolt when we were both sophomores at the University of Washington, both studying business administration. I think what attracted me to him to begin with was that he seemed to be the total opposite of my father. He had no clever lines with women. He always seemed a little awkward and uncertain around them. He was shy and sweet and unsophisticated." She absentmindedly traced the floral pattern in the ceramic tile of the counter as she spoke, fingertips following the delicate blue petals and twining green stems. "He came from a ranch in the central part of the state. The only thing that wasn't very much farm boy about him was that he wanted to get away from the ranch life and see the world. That's why he was studying business adminstration, he said, so he could escape the ranch. He said there was no future on the ranch. We were married in the spring."

"And then he changed from unsophisticated country boy to clever woman chaser?"

Shar shook her head. "No. We had a little off-campus apartment, and I worked part-time for an accounting firm. Then Matt's brother, who had been helping their father run the ranch, got hurt; a horse fell on him. So Matt had to go home on weekends to help out with the ranch work because there wasn't enough money to hire extra help. Then he had to spend all summer working on the ranch, too."

"Did you go with him?"

"No. I wanted to, but we really needed the money I was making at my full-time summer job for the next year's college expenses. We only saw each other a few times all summer. Then, in the fall, his brother was able to work again, but Matt kept going back to the ranch on weekends. A couple of times he didn't get back until the middle of the following week. There was always a sick cow or plowing to be done or something, he said. Finally, after one weekend in November, he just didn't come back at all."

"What happened?"

Shar gave a choked, bitter laugh. "I tried to call him, but he wouldn't come to the phone. Then I got a letter from a girl named Sandy. She said Matt had never been much good at writing letters, and he'd asked her to write it for him. They'd been high school sweethearts, but then he'd got this urge to go to college and see the world. Now he realized he'd made a mistake, that he really was just a country boy and working the ranch was the life he wanted, and he wouldn't be coming back to me or college."

"A man can realize he's made a mistake—"

"He'd been seeing this Sandy all along. When he was telling me he had to stay at the ranch because of a sick cow, it was really to be with her. Sandy was pregnant. They were married as soon as our divorce was final. And I thought he was different from my father! I trusted him. I never had the slightest suspicion he wasn't completely faithful. I'd been fooled by that country-boy drawl and all that awkwardness and innocence . . . and he'd been cheating on me all along, just like my father did to my mother. He didn't even have the courage or decency to tell me himself."

"The situation was a little different from that between your parents, perhaps a little more understandable—"

"You're excusing what Matt did?" Shar challenged.

Tal shook his head heavily. "No."

"And you have no idea how many eager-to-be-unfaithful married men a businesswoman meets in the course of a year," Shar added bitterly.

"I suppose so."

"Then I met you . . . and you were different. I could see it that night at the anniversary party. I tried my damndest to seduce you . . . and you weren't even remotely interested. I was convinced you were that rarest of species, the faithful man." Shar's voice was harsh with resentment that she had been deceived . . . again.

"No doubt this little test had something to do with the way you've avoided letting me know where you live? You were afraid I'd recognize it as the same place I'd driven a certain sexy blonde to."

Shar shrugged. All that seemed long ago and irrelevant now.

"So I was tested and proven trustworthy, and you put me up on some pedestal, far above the ordinary run of men susceptible to the temptations of a pretty face and figure."

He spoke reflectively, almost as if summarizing the points of a business deal under consideration. "Then I did the unforgivable. I tumbled off the pedestal. Apparently it was a rather fatal fall, because now you want nothing to do with me."

Shar didn't argue, though her heart shouted a silent protest. Yes, she wanted to be with him. She wanted to be in his arms, feel his mouth and body on hers, cling to him with all her strength.... But she wouldn't, she vowed fiercely; she would listen only to her clear rational mind.

"Well, let me remind you of something." His reflective tone turned rough and hard. "If I was perched up there on some shining pedestal, far above normal fallible men, it was because you built the pedestal under me, not because I climbed up on it myself. I consider myself a reasonably decent, honest, trustworthy man. I've never set out to deliberately deceive or hurt anyone, man or woman. But I'm no saint. I'm very much human, with all the flaws that implies. And there are at least a couple of women in my past who I'm sure would echo a rather bitter amen to that."

"Then why didn't you succumb when I tried to seduce you at the party... and afterward?" Shar cried. "Why did you make us believe you were so invulnerable to temptation when you're not?"

It was Tal's turn to shrug. "I don't find much appeal in one-night stands anymore. And even less appeal in the type of woman who apparently wants that kind of thing."

"And I don't find much appeal in the type of man who passes himself off as true-blue and faithful... until circumstances make being faithful inconvenient!"

"I see." He turned around and looked at the empty coffee maker, then began preparing more coffee. He measured the ingredients with methodical precision, as if the proportions were of critical importance.

"Has it ever occurred to you," he finally said conversationally, with his back still to her, "that you're in for some rather large disappointments and difficulties in life if the only type of man you're attracted to is one who is being utterly faithful to another woman?"

Shar's denial was instantaneous. "That isn't the way it is—"

"Oh, but it is," he corrected politely. "You wanted me—and don't try to deny it, Shar, you did want me—only until I made it very obvious that I wanted you."

"I don't go around examining all my friends' men to see if they're being faithful, and then wanting them if they are!"

"Grow up, Shar." He whirled to face her, the glass coffeepot still in his hand. "I can sympathize with all the disappointment and disillusionment you've had from unfaithful men in your life, but you're living in an impossible world if you can only be attracted to a man who is being faithful to another woman. It's one hell of a precise recipe for unhappiness."

"No more so than loving a man who has proven he can't be faithful!"

"I can be faithful. I will be faithful. When I've made the commitment to *be* faithful."

"And when will that be?" Shar taunted. "When you're too old to chase anymore? Too debilitated for extracurricular fun and games?"

He slammed the pot to the tile counter, and she was surprised that the glass didn't shatter. He took a deep breath, and then his voice unexpectedly softened a notch. "Shar, why are we doing this to each other? After the things we said and did at the cabin . . ."

Shar closed her eyes, hands clenched defensively at her sides as she battled the seductive memory. He had proved he could be unfaithful, and still she loved him.

"Or was that just another of your little deceits?"

Shar's eyes flew open. She found him looking at her with an odd wary expression on his face.

"You expertly deceived me at the anniversary party. You've deceived me all along about your friendship with Nicole. Maybe everything that happened between us at the cabin, everything you said, was just another of your clever deceptions."

"No." Shar drew back as she breathed the word, shocked by the cold suspicion in his voice. "How could you think that?"

"Maybe making love is just a little fringe benefit you throw in to influence a balky or indecisive client."

Pure fury fueled Shar's shock. How dare he...how could he say something like that after what had happened between them?

Angry denials leaped to Shar's tongue, but she held them back, afraid that even in anger she might reveal her love. And she would not reveal love to a man who thought so little of her, who thought she could ever do what he was suggesting.

She tossed her head defiantly. "Did it work? Have you decided to buy or trade for the cabin?"

Something happened to his face. His mouth twisted and then leveled into a bitter line. He headed for the arched doorway—he was going to stalk out without saying another word.

Then his fist slammed into the expensive woodwork of the arch. "You can take your goddamned cabin and shove it in the ocean for all I care!"

10

THE EXPLOSIVE SLAM of the front door vibrated through the house and sent an echoing shudder through Shar. The ugly accusation and her mocking reply hung in the air. He was gone, saturated with scorn and disgust for her.

What would he do now? No doubt rush back to Nicole. And the eventual result of all this would probably be that Shar would lose both the man she loved and her best friend. No matter what she had said to him about not loving an unfaithful man, it was too late for her. No matter that he had unjustly accused her of something she could never do, she loved him, anyway. And no matter that she cared deeply about Nicole, as well, she could see no way that Nicole would want to remain friends with her if Nicole and Tal got back together.

At the moment Shar was also less self-righteously positive that her taunts about Tal's infidelity were warranted. There had been a convincing ring of truth in his declaration that he could and would be faithful, all the more powerful because he hadn't decorated the statement with fanciful phrases or emotional outcry. He hadn't yet made a real commitment to Nicole, but if he did, he would be forever true.

Dully Shar realized she had done what needed to be done. She had opened the way for the renewal of Tal's relationship with Nicole.

Unless her first worries about Nicole were correct....

Shar tried the number in Palm Springs again. This time it was busy. When she tried again a few minutes later, the maid called Cindy to the phone. Shar made the call seem very casual, asking what Cindy had been doing and getting back her bubbly accounts of horseback riding and swimming. Then Shar asked if Cindy had heard from her mother lately. She had. Nicole had called to say she was going to take a short vacation of her own but would meet Cindy's plane on Sunday. Cindy added that she had also just talked to Tal, which didn't surprise Shar. Evidently he had called the minute he reached home.

Shar unplugged the coffee maker, turned off the lights and locked the door. Unhappy as she was, she could at least feel better about Nicole now. Whatever Nicole was doing, apparently it wasn't life-threatening, because she had assured Cindy she'd meet the plane.

Shar drove home slowly, her own life stretching out bleak and empty ahead of her. Familiar what ifs filled her mind. What if she and Tal had met first? What if she'd simply closed her eyes to Nicole's pain and followed her heart and snatched Tal for herself? Earlier she had refused to listen to her heart, but now it was breaking in anguish and could no longer be ignored.

Yet trying to snatch happiness paid for with Nicole's despair would never have worked. Shar had been through that with her conscience before. So what she had done was right and best, she kept telling herself.

SHAR MUDDLED THROUGH THE REMAINDER of the week, deliberately overscheduling her time with appointments so that there would be less space to think. She got new listings and made a sale, but she couldn't escape a weary feeling that she was simply running faster and faster on an endless, meaningless treadmill. She no longer had any thoughts of buying the cabin herself; the bittersweet memories it held made that impossible. She worried about Nicole, but logic told her that a determined Tal would somehow locate her and they were probably together by now.

Sunday came, and she had an appointment to show a small apartment house that afternoon. But the morning was free. She listlessly cleaned house. Tripod was in the way and underfoot all the time, but she didn't mind. She ran across the jacket she'd tossed in the closet after the Coos Bay trip. The pockets were still heavy with the treasures she'd collected on the beach. They were no longer shimmering jewels, just dull worthless bits of rock and shell. She threw them out . . . all but one rounded stone of pure white. She couldn't say why she saved it. Perhaps because it was one Tal had picked up and tossed to her, and it was all she'd ever have of him. Perhaps because the purity of color symbolized the purity that she wished could have existed in her relationship with Tal.

She was putting clothes in the washer when the doorbell rang. She went to the door, expecting the caller to be the tenants from below with their rent. She found Nicole standing at the door.

Nicole glowed with a radiance Shar hadn't seen in a long time. Her dark eyes sparkled vivaciously, and her cheeks had a flush of color. It meant that she and Tal had gotten back together again, of course, and Shar resolutely forced her mouth into an approving smile.

"You look terrific. But I ought to . . . to take you over my knee and spank you for the way you've worried me!" Shar scolded.

"I know. I'm sorry." The words were contrite, but Nicole's happy smile as she stepped inside wasn't. "I'm on my way to the airport to pick up Cindy, so I just have a minute—I haven't even been home yet! But I wanted to stop by and tell you—"

"I know."

"You do?" Nicole's dark eyes widened in surprise. "And you're not angry? You don't think it was a foolish thing to do?"

"Of course not. I'm sure you and Tal will be very happy."

"Tal?" Nicole repeated the name as if it was vaguely familiar. Then her mouth formed a small O of surprise. "You thought Tal and I got back together?"

"Of course."

Nicole sat down on the sofa, and Tripod began an immediate investigation of the straps on Nicole's purse. Nicole shook her head a little. "Oh, Shar, I know I carried on so when Tal dumped me. All that wailing and crying! But after you talked to me I came up from my low . . . and then down from my high . . . and I really began to examine my feelings. And then I realized that I wasn't so heartbroken after all! I finally figured out that what I actually felt was relief."

"Relief!"

"Yes. Because all along I'd been afraid to admit that I was still in love with Dave. I kept denying it even to myself. But when I finally acknowledged it I took your advice and went after what I *really* wanted."

"Dave?"

Nicole nodded. "I've been with him all week. We're getting back together." She smiled radiantly, then reached over and squeezed Shar's hand. "Don't look so dismayed. I knew you'd disapprove. That's why I didn't have the nerve to tell you what I was planning to do when I sneaked out. And then I wasn't certain that he'd want me back, of course. But he does. He's been miserable. And not only after he and Jill split up but before, as well. He said he'd made a terrible mistake."

"I . . . I guess I'm speechless."

"Shar, I know you're not too fond of Dave, but I never stopped loving him. And I *am* a different person now, just as you said, a stronger person. You helped me find my strengths. Now I'm willing and able to fight for what I want. I'm no longer the kind of woman who will let a man treat her like a dust mop."

Shar smiled in spite of her dismay. "The usual word is doormat."

Nicole smiled back. "Whatever. But I love him, Shar, I really do. Even when I'd pretty well convinced myself I was in love with Tal, there was always this part of me that held back. Which I suppose is one reason we never got around to making love. And surely, if I'd really been in love, I could never have staged that awful seduction test on him! Wasn't that really a terrible thing to do?" She laughed reminiscently, as if the scheme had been just another of their college pranks. "But good old Shar, there you were, loyally standing by me and helping out, no matter what kind of crazy ideas I had."

Shar just shook her head, trying to assimilate it all. Nicole wasn't in love with Tal. Nicole and Dave were getting back together.

"How do you feel about Tal now?" Shar asked finally. "Have you been in touch with him?"

"When we broke up he told me that I'd make some man a wonderful wife someday. And I guess that's the way I feel about him. He'll make some woman a wonderful husband . . . but not me. I can see now that he didn't drop me quite as abruptly as I accused him of doing. He'd been trying to do it for several days, and I just wouldn't let him.

Then he came over that Tuesday morning and finally just plunged in and did what had to be done." As something of an afterthought she added, "I haven't been in touch with him. Maybe I should. He's probably feeling guilty for dumping me, and really it was the best thing that could have happened to me."

Shar's mind skipped over most of Nicole's words, fastening in confusion on the fateful day. "But I thought he came to your house Wednesday afternoon, not very long before you called me."

"Oh, no. I'd been trying to call you since the previous day. I'd really worked myself into a state, of course, by the time I finally got hold of you. Where were you, anyway?" she added curiously.

Shar hesitated, one part of her wanting to pour out everything, another part unwilling to intrude on Nicole's happiness with messy details of her own problems. She'd probably share it all with Nicole someday, but now she simply said vaguely, "Oh, just another business trip."

Nicole glanced at her watch. "I have to run. Shar, thanks for everything. Thanks for being there when I needed you . . . *again* . . . and thanks for the advice. And don't be too hard on Dave, please? I love him, and when you really love a man, you love him imperfections and all. Who knows, maybe there are even some advantages to a man who has strayed and returned! He knows the pastures out there aren't really so green after all." After a pause she added irrepressibly, "And I just may do something with that idea of starting a catering service, too!"

Shar wasn't sure she shared Nicole's optimistic philosophy about men who strayed, but she gave her friend a congratulatory hug. Then Nicole was gone, leaving behind a faint scent of seductive perfume. Not, Shar noted, the kind of light innocent cologne she'd worn when seeing Tal.

Tripod plopped into Shar's lap, and Shar absentmindedly stroked the kitten's fur, which was already growing lush and glossy. Reuniting Nicole and Dave certainly wasn't what she had intended with her advice that Nicole go after what she wanted, but perhaps it really was what was right for Nicole. If Nicole's radiance was any indication, Dave was the man for her. Shar fervently hoped so.

And if Tal and Nicole weren't getting back together... Shar felt a stirring of hope, a surge of excitement. That changed everything! Adding volatile fuel to Shar's hope was the realization that her accusations hadn't been justified. Tal had never made any real commitment to Nicole, as he had said, and what tenuous understanding there had been had ended *before* his night with Shar at the cabin.

She had simply assumed that Tal had gone to Nicole's house after the trip, during the time Shar was delayed by that flat tire. But he had ended his relationship with Nicole before the trip. That was why he had almost missed the plane, why he'd seemed so preoccupied. The crucial timing put a whole new light on his actions. Before the flight to Coos Bay he hadn't known the trip to the cabin would turn into an overnight affair, but he'd wanted to do the honorable thing and end one relationship before becoming involved in a new one. He hadn't been unfaithful to Nicole; he'd played fair.

Hope suddenly plummeted, shot down by the knowledge that even if Tal and Nicole weren't getting back together, he'd never return to her. Not after the things they'd said to each other. She cringed at the memory of his scorn when he'd stalked away from her.

But she could go to him . . . explain.

Why should he believe her? She'd deceived him too many times, proved too convincingly that she wasn't to be trusted with love or friendship. She'd teased and deceived him at the masquerade party. She'd deceived him by never revealing her longtime friendship with Nicole. No doubt he had even read something meaningful into her implying that she was "protected," and thus prepared for an unexpected night of intimacy on a business trip.

Shar desperately wished she could just escape for a few days, go someplace where she wouldn't have to talk to clients and smile, wouldn't have to pretend her heart wasn't shriveling inside her. Yet she really didn't want to be alone, battered by thoughts and emotions. . . .

In the days that followed she found tears streaming down her cheeks at odd moments. She feigned a newly acquired allergy to explain her red-rimmed eyes, and Lil solicitously provided antihistamine capsules.

What she really wanted to do, Shar realized unhappily, was crawl into a dark hole and pull it in after her. She knew that was no way to face troubles, no way to solve problems, yet the desire to simply fade into numb oblivion was there. She talked to Nicole on the phone several times. Dave wasn't home yet but would be in a few days. But even in her new-found happiness, Nicole sensed something wasn't right with Shar and kept asking what it was.

"Just this silly allergy I've developed," Shar would say brightly to explain a hoarseness in her voice. "Just a number of business matters on my mind," she'd say to explain a tendency to forget something Nicole had just told her.

The following week she included the coast cabin in a newspaper advertisement of properties for sale or trade. There were several calls about it, and one woman, Mrs. Patterson, said she and her husband definitely wanted to look at the cabin. She said they were going to be in the Coos Bay area the following weekend. Could they see it then?

Shar had no desire to go anywhere near the cabin again. She suggested the woman and her husband just drive out and see it themselves, but the woman insisted that she wanted to inspect the interior of the cabin. Finally Shar made an impulsive decision. The weather was supposed to be nice on the coast this weekend. She'd drive down to Coos Bay to show the cabin, then just keep on following the coast highway and spend a few days visiting with her mother and Clyde in San Francisco. Her mother was a vivacious chatterer; it would be nearly impossible to think too deeply about Tal when she was with her mother.

Shar gave the woman directions to the cabin, and they arranged a late-afternoon meeting for Saturday. She told Lil she'd be away a few days. She might even consider moving to San Francisco, she decided vaguely. She could look around and make some inquiries while she was there.

She arranged for her tenants who lived in the main portion of the house to look after Tripod, then called Nicole to say she'd be away for a few days. She packed enough clothes for a week or so and dressed in a comfortable zipper-front jump suit for the long drive. She intended to make it at least as far as the California line before stopping for the night.

A SPRING RAIN WAS DRIZZLING on the city when she drove out of town Saturday morning, but it was a drenching downpour by the time she reached Coos Bay. So much for favorable weather reports, she thought dispiritedly. She was half-inclined to skip driving to the cabin and head directly down the coast; on a day such as this the clients probably wouldn't even show up. A characteristic sense of responsibilty made her sigh and go on, however. She wasn't one to give her word and then not keep it.

The gate was open when she reached the narrow lane that led to the cabin. The Pattersons must already have arrived.

But the small sports car parked beside the A-frame cabin looked oddly familiar. . . . She realized why as a tall figure stepped out from beneath the protection of the porch. Tal!

For a moment she thought she must be imagining him, but the broad-shouldered lanky figure that strolled toward her was no fantasy. He was all reality, all coolly confident male, his smile an incongruously brilliant flash in the slanting rain.

She rolled down the window but, wary of a certain predatory aura about him, didn't get out of the car. "What are you doing here?"

He walked up to the car, leaned down and peered through the open window. "I thought I'd take another look at the cabin. There were so many distractions the last time I was here." He smiled again, lazily, as if they were having a leisurely discussion over cocktails. Rain battered his bare head, but he didn't seem to notice.

"I don't know how you happened to choose this particular time to come here, but I'm here on business. I'm meeting clients here." Shar's tone was as unfriendly as the cold rain. Rather hastily she added, "A married couple."

"I know. Mr. and Mrs. Patterson."

She couldn't hide her surprise. "Who told you that?"

"You're not the only one who can plan clever deceptions, you know. With modest pride I must admit that *I* am Mr. and Mrs. Patterson." With a mocking flourish he swept one arm to his waist and bowed slightly, his dark hair flinging a sprinkling of droplets into her face.

She brushed distractedly at the wet drops. "But you can't be! I don't believe it. I talked with Mrs. Patterson herself—"

"My secretary. A lovely middle-aged lady who adores romantic intrigue. I told her we'd had a lovers' quarrel, and she was delighted to help patch it up by participating in this small deception."

"You had no right—"

"You're angry. And here I thought you'd be intrigued by my creativity." His mouth was exaggeratedly downcast.

"I'm leaving."

Shar reached to turn the key in the ignition, but his hand clamped around her wrist. With his other hand he removed the keys. He held the key ring just out of reach when she grabbed for it.

"I want to see the cabin again," he said.

"Then go see it! You know where the key is hidden."

"I want you to show it to me again." Idly he twirled her key ring around his forefinger, his eyes on hers. "You're not getting the car keys back until you do, you know."

Shar glanced back at the puddled lane overhung with wet drooping branches. She'd tried that escape route once; it hadn't worked. And she knew he was capable of carrying out his threat.

Furtively she eyed his car. Would he have thought to remove the keys from it?

"Why are you doing this?" she demanded, stalling for time. If she could just get to his car . . .

"I had second thoughts about the cabin. It's really a lovely, secluded trysting spot, and you did make it plain that my actions constituted cold-blooded unfaithfulness. It's just the sort of place every unfaithful man should have for clandestine meetings."

Cold-blooded? That was hardly how Shar would have described the night they'd spent here together. But what she stiffly said was "Nicole and Dave are getting back together."

Tal made no comment on the irrelevancy of the statement. "I know. I called to make sure she was okay."

"How nice of you."

"That's me, Mr. Nice Guy." He turned toward the cabin, her car keys still firmly in hand. A certain wicked glitter in his eyes belied his words. "Coming?"

Shar tossed a jacket over her shoulders and got out of the car. She formed a quick plan. She would accompany him to the porch, find the hidden key and hand it to him. While he was unlocking the cabin door, she'd make a quick dash for his car. She wasn't certain exactly what she was afraid of here. Surely he wouldn't actually force himself on her. Yet there was a menacing air of unpredictability about him, a sizzling but leashed virility. Who would have thought he'd come up with a devious scheme like this?

Her plan went awry from the first. When they reached the porch she found he had already unlocked the door. He propelled her inside with a steel grip on her elbow. A blazing fire crackled in the fireplace, and the cabin had a warm cozy intimacy that did nothing to alter her apprehension.

"I got cold while I was waiting for you, so I made myself at home," he explained. He tossed his raincoat on the sofa. "I also found an adjustment on the fireplace damper that puts a little more heat into the cabin."

"How nice. And this?" She pointed to a bottle of champagne in an ice bucket on the plank counter.

"I wanted to show my appeciation for your charming fringe benefits. There are also a couple of nice steaks to broil on the fire later. And I remembered that you don't care for sardines for breakfast, so I brought ham and eggs."

He was toying with her, Shar realized furiously. Yet at the moment she couldn't think of anything to do about it. He was careful to keep himself between her and the door.

"You said you wanted to see the cabin. Very well, what would you like to see that you didn't see last time? The plumbing?" She threw open the cabinet door below the chipped porcelain sink. "Guaranteed for two weeks or one tryst, whichever comes first."

"Sounds good to me."

She opened the door to the tiny bathroom. "Equipped with all the modern conveniences, of course. I'm sure you'll notice that the shower, though small, is ample for two friendly adults."

"My only regret is that the electricity is still shut off, so there's no running water, and these two friendly adults won't be able to engage in any water-based fun and games."

"No scrub and tell? What a pity." She slammed the bathroom door. "Sleeping quarters are upstairs. But you've already seen them."

"I think there's a leak in the roof over the loft. If you'd be so kind as to take a look . . ."

Shar climbed the steep stairs to he dimly lit loft, her back rigid as she gripped the rough wooden rail. There was indeed a rhythmic plop-plop of water dripping into a can. She'd heard it the other time, as well.

"Yes, I believe you're right. There's definitely a leak. Perhaps a bargaining point if you want to deal on the cabin."

"You can hear it much better from here—" With a casual but commanding grip on her shoulder he turned her so that she was facing away from the bed, and a moment later she found herself sprawled across the mattress, pinned beneath his body.

For a few moments there were no sounds but their muffled gasps and grunts and the creaks of the old bed as she struggled silently to escape the crush of his body. She twisted and squirmed, got one knee free only to have it recaptured under the hard length of his leg. She ignored the feel of her breasts pushing against his chest as she writhed from side to side. He had her arms pinned to her sides, but she managed to dig her thumbs savagely into the taut muscles just inside his hipbones.

He rose slightly to look down at her. "If you're trying to turn me on, it's working." His tone was pleasantly conversational, but he was breathing hard from the struggle, and his eyes were darkened in a way that warned he wasn't merely making conversation. The hard thrust of his pelvis against her legs emphasized his arousal.

Shar's struggles abruptly ceased. She held herself rigidly stiff, so motionless that she was hardly breathing beneath him. She'd lost her jacket in the scuffle, and the zipper of the jump suit angled across one breast.

"That turns me on, too," he whispered. "Everything about you turns me on." The whisper deepened until it was almost a growl, a rough blend of anger and resentment and desire.

Shar gritted her teeth and refused to respond. She kept her eyes focused on a stained spot on the ceiling over his left shoulder, aloof, as if oblivious to the weight of his body and the imprisonment of his arms and legs.

Yet she wasn't oblivious to him . . . and she knew he was as aware of that fact as she was. Her heart hammered from something more than the efforts of the struggle, and she desperately feared that if he once broke through the stiff shell of her resistance, he'd find only hot welcome within.

She clenched her knees more tightly together, fiercely determined not to let that happen, not to let the demands of her body overwhelm the defenses of her mind.

But her defenses were under attack from all sides.

He kissed the corners of her clamped mouth. He rained kisses over her cheeks and temples and eyes, all the while moving his body against hers in intimately suggestive rhythms. His mouth dipped to her ear, and he teased the lobe with the provocative caress of his tongue.

"Like that?" he whispered. "Or perhaps this is better...." His tongue entered the whorl of her ear, shooting a tingle through her body.

But still she held herself rigid, gaze and thoughts concentrated on the ceiling stain, as if it were a protective talisman, all that kept her from responding to him with abandon.

Leisurely his mouth proceeded down her throat, kissing and nibbling with seductive expertise. He paused at the pulse point, absorbing the wild beat, then moved lower, following the silken cords to the hollow at the base of her throat. His tongue circled and filled the creamy hollow, and she was slowly, surely spinning around the pivot point of his tongue.

He gripped the tab on the zipper of her jump suit with his teeth and gave it a tug to test its resistance. There was none. She tried to grab the zipper, but her hands were still pinned at her sides, and the leisurely descent continued. The gap widened, the fabric pulled taut by the swollen throb of her breasts. The white lace of her bra gleamed in the opening, the curve of flesh lush above the low cut.

She felt her rigid nipples straining for release, yet anger overrode the desire he aroused in her, and green fire leaped from her eyes as his pelvis pressed ever deeper against her.

"Why are you doing this? Why did you dupe me into coming here? I'm sure there must be any number of women willing to crawl into bed with you without your having to resort to trickery."

The provocative pressure retreated, and unexpectedly his forehead rested against hers. "I did it this way because I knew damn well you'd never talk to me if I simply tried to phone or see you. I may not be the most astute of men, but I'm aware that a woman isn't going to feel kindly toward a man who said the things I did. Not that I can blame you, because we both know there isn't a dime's worth of truth in the accusation I made."

He lifted his head to look directly into her eyes. "I'm sorry, Shar. It was a cruel and unfair thing to say. I was angry and . . . hurt. But that didn't give me any right to insult you."

Shar felt resistance softening within her, a treacherous weakness that wanted to accept his apology and forget everything but the desire surging through her. But he *had* tricked her into coming here, and in spite of the apology she was still trapped beneath his body.

"So why didn't you just call up and apologize?" she demanded stubbornly.

"How much effect would that have had on a woman who's convinced I'm also a dedicated woman chaser, unfaithful to the core? You'd have hung up on me as soon as you heard my voice." He touched the corner of her mouth with soft lips. "And if I weren't holding you down, you'd already have walked out on me here."

"I suppose I may have been . . . a little harsh on you," Shar admitted. "Nicole told me you'd broken up with her before we came to the cabin."

"And Nicole told me that party deception was her idea. So why did you let me think you'd deceived me about the feelings that passed between us here? Why didn't you deny my unfair accusation?"

When Shar didn't respond to the question, he said softly, "I think I know the answer."

Shar simply eyed him warily.

"You thought your best friend was in love with me, and you're too . . . too noble a person to steal a man from your best friend. So you did the only thing you could do. Let me become angry at you so that I'd run back to her."

Noble? After the things she'd done. Oh, no. Shar shook her head a little helplessly. "I was angry and hurt, too. Shocked that you could think that of me. Overwhelmed with guilt . . ."

"I'm sorry," he repeated softly. "But if you felt guilty about coming between Nicole and me, you wasted a lot of emotional energy. You were perhaps the catalyst that made me see what a mistake marriage to Nicole would have been, but Nicole and I would have broken up, anyway, sooner or later. She's a wonderful, sweet woman, but if I was going to fall in love with her, it would have happened before I got involved with you. Just *wanting* to fall in love with someone isn't enough. We're too different." He glanced around almost idly. The late-afternoon light was fading, and shadows from the fire danced on the ceiling. "Nicole would hate this place."

"It's nice, really." Shar became aware of the cozy patter of rain on the roof, the pleasant scent of the wood fire crackling below. "All it needs is a little tender loving care."

"Don't we all?" he asked with a soft laugh. Then, "Is that a sales pitch? If it is, you needn't bother. I'm already sold on the cabin."

"I can write up an offer." Shar tried to sit up, but Tal held her to the bed.

"There's just one condition."

"What's that?" she asked.

"We'll have the electricity and water turned on. We'll bring blankets and music, lay in a supply of food, enough so we won't have to leave the cabin or get out of bed for a week—"

"I thought you understood. There aren't any fringe benefits!" Shar said with a flash of anger. His apology was worthless! She got her hands up and braced them against his shoulders as she twisted to aim her knee at his groin.

"—And then we'll spend our honeymoon here."

Shar stopped in midwrithe, her astonished gaze meeting his. "Honeymoon!"

Offhandedly he added, "That's a marriage proposal, in case I didn't make it clear."

"Proposal!" she echoed. Her bent knee collapsed.

"Sweetheart, I'm sorry if I've disappointed you. I'm sorry if I didn't treat your friend the way you thought I should have. I'm sorry we haven't had a...a normal courtship, with flowers and dates and romance." He looked down at her and shook his head regretfully. "But I love you. And I want to marry you. If you can just trust me enough, let me prove to you that I'll be faithful...."

"Love you. Marry you." The words echoed in Shar's head. She examined them, disbelievingly at first, then with growing wonderment.

"Aren't you going to answer me?" he asked.

"Who needs food and electricity and blankets?" she whispered recklessly. "Don't you already know that I'm the woman who can live on love?"

"And I'm the man who's been starving for lack of it."

His mouth dipped to hers, his lips covering hers with sweet tenderness and gentle fire. Shar's eyes drifted shut; she was floating like a bubble in a dark world encompassed by his body and limbs and mouth. Her arms crept up to encircle his neck. His tongue slipped past her parted lips, and his knee nudged her unresisting legs apart. He fit himself lovingly into the yielding curves and hollows of her body.

"I love you," he whispered fiercely. "Even before I knew I was in love with you, I stopped wanting any other woman."

"Mr. Nice Guy," she teased softly.

"You think so?" He buried his pelvis hard against her, driving her into the soft mattress. "Still think so?"

"Oh, yes. That's very nice."

"It would be nicer if there weren't so many clothes between us." He shifted to a kneeling position over her and reached for the zipper tab. He hesitated, hand poised above her breast. "Do I dare?"

She gave him a lazy-lidded smile. "I guess you'll just have to try it and see."

He reached again for the zipper, and she caught his hand. She brought it to her lips and kissed each fingertip and then the damp palm. And then she leisurely lowered the zipper herself.

He watched for a moment before snatching the metal tab out of her hand. "You're too slow," he muttered. He yanked the zipper down until it encountered the barrier of the belt at her waist. Then he reverently spread the fabric like a frame around her breasts, and his hands cupped the outer curves still covered with the pristine white bra.

"And so are you...slow," she whispered back. She shrugged out of the upper half of the jump suit, and their hands collided as they both fumbled for the bra fastener behind her back.

He caressed her naked breasts, stroking and cupping the lush curves with his palms as his fingertips played sensuous havoc with the rigid peaks. Sparks shot back through his wrist and arm, shot forward into the yearning depths of her body. She unbuttoned his shirt, as eager for the touch of his skin as he was for hers. She ran her hands across his sleek taut skin and hard muscles.

Despite the obvious readiness of his body, he gave a thought to their surroundings. "We could go somewhere else," he offered huskily. "Somewhere that isn't quite so primitive."

"Did I say I objected to primitive?" she asked, challenging him with a sultry rotation of hips.

"You'd better be careful, or it isn't only the cabin that will be primitive—"

In answer she tugged on the front of his shirt. She had intended merely to pull out the shirttail, but a button pinged against the floor. She stared at the dangling threads from which it had torn loose.

He grinned. "I think there's a bit of the primitive inside my passionate angel, too." He straightened his shoulders and thrust his chest forward. "Care to rip a few more buttons?"

"Why not?" Shar answered recklessly.

But she didn't get the chance because he tossed the shirt away, and then they were both fumbling with buckles and zippers and barriers of fabric. When they were both naked he kissed her again, the touch an intoxicating blend of fire and tenderness, giving and demanding. Shar was no longer a drifting bubble; now she was all warm eager flesh, conscious of desires of a very specific, basic nature. She felt a wild blossoming of pleasure, sensed that any more could send her spinning out of control.

But there was more . . . much, much more. . . .

Tal joined his body with hers, gently but firmly. "I love you," he whispered, and he repeated the words with each stroke. "I love you . . . love you . . . love you. . . ." And the loving words joined with the rhythm of his body loving her and became one with it. The words echoed within her, becoming a part of her, too, and she joined him in the joyous litany, repeating the words not just with her whisper but with heart and soul, as well.

It would have been enough for her just to have this, but there was still more. There was the reaching, the soaring . . . and then the final thunderclap, the tumultuous welding of two explosions and his "I love you!" a shout not a whisper.

Long moments later he roused himself enough to ask, "I hope that was a yes to my proposal?"

Their bodies were warm and damp. Shar twisted a strand of his tousled hair around her fingertip. Oh, yes, yes! But . . .

"I love you," she whispered. "I want to marry you. . . ."

He heard the hesitation in the soft statement. "But?" he prodded.

"I—I'm not the tranquil domestic package you thought you wanted. I love my job, and sometimes I work crazy hours, and I'm not much on fancy cooking or scrupulous housekeeping—"

"Can you tell the difference between a vacuum cleaner and a washing machine?" he demanded. "Distinguish between a boiled egg and a fried one?"

"Yes . . . on a good day."

"Good—so can I. We can share those chores." He kissed her on the nose, and then his voice went husky. "Shar, I love *you*, whatever you are. I wouldn't change a single thing about you." He hesitated before adding tentatively, "Although I guess I was hoping you might find time to provide the 'and Son' to make it 'O'Neal and Son Construction' again." He broke off thoughtfully. "Or 'O'Neal and Daughter.' I'm not fussy."

"I think I could work that in." Suggestively she added, "With a little help from you."

"Anytime," he whispered lovingly. "Anytime."

Harlequin Temptation

COMING NEXT MONTH

Harlequin "Super Celebration"
SWEEPSTAKES

NEW PRIZES—NEW PRIZE FEATURES & CHOICES—MONTHLY

1. To enter the sweepstakes, follow the instructions outlined on the Center Insert Card. Alternate means of entry, NO PURCHASE NECESSARY, you may also enter by mailing your name, address and birthday on a plain 3″ x 5″ piece of paper to: In U.S.A.: Harlequin "Super Celebration" Sweepstakes, P.O. Box 1867, Buffalo, N.Y. 14240-1867. In Canada: Harlequin "Super Celebration" Sweepstakes, P.O. Box 2800, 5170 Yonge Street, Postal Station A, Willowdale, Ontario M2N 6J3.

2. Winners will be selected in random drawings from all entries received. All prizes will be awarded. These prizes are in addition to any free gifts which might be offered. Versions of this sweepstakes with different prizes may appear in other presentations by TorStar and their affiliates. The maximum value of the prizes offered is $8,000.00. Winners selected will receive the prize offered from their prize package.

3. The selection of winners will be conducted under the supervision of Marden-Kane, an independent judging organization. By entering the sweepstakes, each entrant accepts and agrees to be bound by these rules and the decision of the judges which shall be final and binding. Odds of winning are dependent upon the total number of entries received. Taxes, if any, are the sole responsibility of the winners. Prizes are not transferable. This sweepstakes is scheduled to appear in Retail Outlets of Harlequin Books during the period of June 1986 to December 1986. All entries must be received by January 31st, 1987. The drawing will take place on or about March 1st, 1987 at the offices of Marden-Kane, Lake Success, New York. For Quebec (Canada) residents, any litigation regarding the running of this sweepstakes and the awarding of prizes must be submitted to La Regie de Lotteries et Course du Quebec.

4. This presentation offers the prizes as illustrated on the Center Insert Card.

5. This offer is open to residents of the U.S., and Canada, 18 years or older, except employees of TorStar, its affilliates, subsidiaries, Marden-Kane and all other agencies and persons connected with conducting this sweepstakes. All Federal, State and local laws apply. Void where prohibited or restricted by law. Winners will be notified by mail and may be required to execute an affidavit of eligibility and release which must be returned within 14 days after notification. Winners consent to the use of their name, photograph and/or likeness for advertising and publicity in conjunction with this and similar promotions without additional compensation. One prize per family or household. Canadian winners will be required to answer a skill testing question.

6. For a list of our most recent prize winners, send a stamped, self-addressed envelope to: WINNERS LIST, c/o Marden-Kane, P.O. Box 525, Sayreville, NJ 08872.

No Lucky Number needed to win!

ATTRACTIVE, SPACE SAVING BOOK RACK

Display your most prized novels on this handsome and sturdy book rack. The hand-rubbed walnut finish will blend into your library decor with quiet elegance, providing a practical organizer for your favorite hard-or soft-covered books.

Only $9.95

Approximately 16" x 8" when assembled

Assembles in seconds!

To order, rush your name, address and zip code, along with a check or money order for $10.70 ($9.95 plus 75¢ postage and handling) (New York residents add appropriate sales tax), payable to *Harlequin Reader Service* to:

In the U.S.

Harlequin Reader Service
Book Rack Offer
901 Fuhrmann Blvd.
P.O. Box 1325
Buffalo, NY 14269-1325

Offer not available in Canada.

BKR–1

Two exciting genres in one great promotion!

Harlequin Gothic and Regency Romance Specials!

GOTHICS—
romance and love growing in the shadow of impending doom...

REGENCIES—
lighthearted romances set in England's Regency period (1811-1820)

SEPTEMBER TITLES

Gothic Romance	Regency Romance
CASTLE MALICE Marilyn Ross	THE TORPID DUKE Pauline York
LORD OF HIGH CLIFF MANOR Irene M. Pascoe	THE IMPERILED HEIRESS Janice Kay Johnson
THE DEVEREAUX LEGACY Carolyn G. Hart	THE GRAND STYLE Leslie Reid

Be sure not to miss these new and intriguing stories ...224 pages of wonderful reading!

Available in September wherever paperback books are sold, or send your name, address and zip or postal code, along with a check or money order for $2.25 U.S./$2.50 Canada for each book ordered, plus 75¢ postage and handling, payable to Harlequin Reader Service to:

Harlequin Reader Service

In the U.S.
901 Fuhrmann Blvd.
P.O. Box 1397,
Buffalo, NY 14240
U.S.A.

In Canada
P.O. Box 2800, Postal Station A
5170 Yonge Street
Willowdale, Ontario M2N 6J3
Canada

CR-B-1